"I can't resist you."

"Oh, yes," Lexy whispered in a voice she barely recognized.

She felt the light stubble of his beard as he kissed his slow way up to her ear, then murmured, "You steal my breath away."

His clever thief's hands moved, tracing the front of her robe to the sash, which he untied, pulling the edges apart and revealing her lacy bra and panties.

The robe fell to the floor and it was his turn to make an incomprehensible sound, half sigh, half moan. "I want you."

Her body was on fire. She felt as much on display as the emeralds she wore, and the experience was intoxicating. "I want you, too."

He touched her carefully, like a man who appreciates art and takes what he wants without asking permission. *Where was this leading?*

He was fully dressed standing behind her, dark and serious but for the gleaming eyes that showed how close to the edge of passion he was.

"This is a terrible idea," she said.

"I know." And then he turned her around and pulled her into his arms, kissing her so hard she felt the breath squeeze out of her.

Blaze

Dear Reader,

What is it about a thief hero that we love so much? Is it that he will take what he wants without asking—and that just might be the heroine? Is it that he's a man who lives life on his own terms and makes his own rules? Of course, the thief hero is not some thug who hits little old ladies and steals their purses. No. Our kind of thief would risk his life to protect that little old lady and make sure she got her purse back. He's elegant, smooth, only takes things from not very nice people who can afford to lose the stuff. He's a pro. He's Cary Grant in *It Takes a Thief*, he's Robert Wagner in *To Catch a Thief*, he's Pierce Brosnan in *The Thomas Crown Affair*.

He is, in a word, dreamy. Tough, smart, a born rule-breaker, and yet the right woman can tame him. Mmmm. *Too Hot to Handle* is my first attempt at writing a thief hero. I've always wanted to and never had the story. Until now.

I hope you enjoy Lexy and Charlie as much as I did. As always, you can come visit me at www.nancywarren.net.

Happy reading,

Nancy Warren

Nancy Warren

TOO HOT TO HANDLE

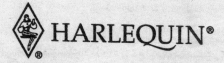

TORONTO • NEW YORK • LONDON
AMSTERDAM • PARIS • SYDNEY • HAMBURG
STOCKHOLM • ATHENS • TOKYO • MILAN • MADRID
PRAGUE • WARSAW • BUDAPEST • AUCKLAND

Recycling programs
for this product may
not exist in your area.

ISBN-13: 978-0-373-79530-7

TOO HOT TO HANDLE

ABOUT THE AUTHOR

USA TODAY bestselling author Nancy Warren lives in the Pacific Northwest where her hobbies include walking her border collie in the rain and searching out unusual jewelry. She's the author of more than thirty novels and novellas for Harlequin and has won numerous awards. Visit her at www.nancywarren.net.

Books by Nancy Warren

HARLEQUIN BLAZE

19—LIVE A LITTLE!
47—WHISPER
57—BREATHLESS
85—BY THE BOOK
114—STROKE OF MIDNIGHT "Tantalizing"
209—PRIVATE RELATIONS
275—INDULGE
389—FRENCH KISSING
452—UNDER THE INFLUENCE
502—POWER PLAY

HARLEQUIN SUPERROMANCE

1390—THE TROUBLE WITH TWINS

HARLEQUIN NASCAR

SPEED DATING
TURN TWO

This is for my readers.

Thank you for your kind messages
and for reading the books I love to write.

With love, Nancy

1

LEXY DRAKE LOVED CONTRASTS. Delicate with bold, hot colors with cold, new mixed with old.

Hard rock music played as she peered through the binocular magnifier and looped a string of molten gold with infinite care around a ruby.

She loved every one of the creations that were slowly making her rich—this one a pair of wedding rings for a young couple who'd come to her with his grandmother's rings and a brooch that had been in her family so long no one knew its provenance.

Lexy would transform the old and forgotten into the new and now. It was the best kind of recycling, combining art, family history and love.

She worked alone, which was how she liked it. But never in silence. Her work might be delicate but her music provided much-needed contrast. Hard-driving rock and roll hammered the air around her. She'd have preferred to let the music reverberate off the walls, but since her tiny studio was tucked behind her SoHo store, she kept the volume low.

With the metal soft, she had a little time to bend it to

her will, but only a little. With a final twist, she had the look she wanted; a bold swirl of gold twining around a ruby.

A sudden prickling at the back of her neck told her she was no longer alone.

She turned sharply in time to surprise a man standing in the doorway. The way his gaze suddenly rose, she suspected she'd been shaking her booty in time to the music and her latest customer had stopped to watch her swaying hips.

He didn't look at all embarrassed to have been caught staring at her gyrations. If anything he appeared—interested—that would have to be the word.

"There's a salesclerk out front if you need help." It was rare for a customer to bumble back here to her private work space, but it happened.

"She's busy. So I followed the music."

"Oh." She picked up the remote and punched down the volume on her iPod. "I should hire more staff now we're getting so busy, but I haven't got around to it. Sorry."

"Don't be. It's fascinating to watch a master craftsman at work." He spoke in that perma-bored drawl with the crisp inflections she'd come to associate with the rich. She was pretty sure he'd been studying her ass—not her master craftsman hands—but he was a potential customer so she didn't call him on it.

Probably a lucrative customer, too. His handmade suit and shiny leather loafers screamed *Daddy owns a bank,* while his tie had one of those crests from a fancy Ivy League school. She could never keep them straight, wasn't interested enough to bother.

"I'm Charles Pendegraff III," he told her in that snooty tone, holding out his hand to shake hers.

"And I'm Alexandra Drake. Lexy." An imp inside her who would probably make sure she ended up broke, added, "The one and only."

His gaze sharpened on hers and she was struck by the gleam of powerful intelligence behind the laziness. The impression was gone in a second. He said, "I see you're working on a ring. I'm thinking of having one commissioned, myself. Do you mind if I take a look?"

"Sure." He had money to burn and she had self-defense skills that would flatten him in a New York minute if he tried anything. He strolled toward her and she figured he might be rich, but he wasn't idle. When he moved, his slacks molded around powerful thighs and as the blazer shifted she got the impression of a broad, muscular chest.

She loved contrasts and he seemed to have enough to be interesting. The lazy speaking voice was at odds with the sharp green eyes; the soft manicured hands didn't match the hard planes of his face.

And when he moved closer she felt the punch of his forceful sexuality.

Wowza.

"How did you hear about my studio?" she asked him. She nearly always started with a little market research and in this case a chance to distract her from the instant and powerful attraction she was experiencing.

"One of the fellows I play polo with, Jeremy Thurston, had you design an amulet for his mother. I bumped into her when she was wearing it at one of those tedious fundraisers. She was dull. The bracelet was stunning."

"Thanks." She remembered the piece, of course. She remembered them all.

"So, I'd heard of you, but I hadn't imagined you'd be

so young. And somehow one never imagines a jeweler as sexy, now why is that?"

"Oh, well…" She could not think of a thing to say. Lexy was rarely thrown off her stride, and getting hit on wasn't a completely foreign experience, so to be tongue-tied in front of this stranger was infuriating. But then she rarely felt the punch of attraction quite this strongly. And never from a guy with a number after his name.

No wonder she was speechless.

"Let me show you what I'm doing here," she said, deciding to ignore the sexy comment and reaching a hand toward the design she'd penned. "I'm combining elements—antique gold, a splash of platinum, those tiny rubies and the diamond solitaire, it's sort of my signature, you see—"

She stopped when he suddenly reached for her hand, taking it in his. "You've hurt yourself," he said, pointing to a red patch on her index finger.

"Oh, that's nothing, I burned myself on the soldering iron. I got careless."

She tried to pull away from the intimate warmth of her hand resting in his, but with a strength that surprised her, he prevented her. "Do you have a first-aid kit?"

"Yes, but I can't have cream or bandages on my fingers. I need them to do my work."

His gaze rose to meet hers and she thought he had the most amazing eyes she'd ever seen. "Then I'll use an old home remedy of my grandmother's." His words licked at her, soft, caressing. Intimate. "I'll kiss it better."

Her hand fluttered in his. She felt it, knew he must have felt the instinctive movement, too; she was completely annoyed by her reaction, but she didn't yank her hand away, either. She watched him raise her fingers slowly to his lips. Felt the lightest whisper of a kiss land on the sore spot and then he returned her hand to the worktable.

"I—um." She completely forgot what she was going to say.

He glanced through her magnifier at the ring. "This is exquisite."

"Thank you. What kind of a ring are you looking for, Mr. Pendegraff?"

"It's Charlie. And I need an engagement ring."

She blinked. "An engagement ring?"

"Yes." He raised his head and glanced at her. His green eyes were like cloudy emeralds, with too many occlusions to make them gemstone worthy, but it was the dark lines, the faults that made them so magnetic.

"You're getting married?"

"Yes."

She couldn't believe the balls of this man. He was kissing the fingers of the woman he wanted to design his wedding rings?

But then she reminded herself of one of her mother's favorite sayings. "The rich have different rules than the rest of us."

That was why she stayed away from them.

"Penelope and I are getting married in September. That's six months from now. Lots of time."

"I see." Ice coated her tone. "Well, if you'd like to come back out front, I'll show you what's in stock. All the designs are original, of course." Lexy was a certified gemologist and she'd apprenticed with a designer in London. When she'd returned to the States, she'd been unwilling to work in one of those design factories that turn out diamond solitaires and wedding bands by the thousand. So, she'd gone out on her own, building herself a perfect little studio in SoHo, a live/work loft that meant she and her livelihood were never far apart, and her commute was less than a minute.

One of the things she loved about New York was how quickly word spread when somebody found a new designer. She'd gone from complete obscurity, to a few select jewelers selling her unique creations, to becoming the go-to designer for wealthy trendsetters in less than two years.

She was so hot that men like Charles Pendegraff III came slumming in order to get his bride the trendiest engagement ring possible.

"Or, I could have something designed, just for me?"

"And for your fiancée. Yes."

As luck would have it, when she returned him to the storefront, her assistant, Amanda, was returning a ring tray to its display case. Her customer was walking out the door with one of their signature boxes made from recycled metal.

"Oh, good. Amanda's free now. Amanda? Would you help Mr. Pendegraff? He's looking for a ring. Goodbye, Mr. Pendegraff, and best of luck with the wedding."

"Bye, Lexy." He stuck out his hand and what could she do but return his clasp? Amusement lurked deep in his eyes as he gazed down at her. "I look forward to seeing you again."

She mumbled something inarticulate and retreated to her work space, shaking her head.

Poor Penelope.

CHARLIE STRODE AROUND a bundle of yellow garbage bags piled on the sidewalk, dodging tourists as he checked out the entire block around Alexandra Drake Designs.

As he took careful note of his Broome Street sur- roundings, snapping a few discreet photos, he pondered the nature of the woman he was about to steal from.

A woman of contrasts. Contrasts that intrigued him. When he'd first walked in, casually, a customer looking for some information, delighted to find the single sales- clerk busy, he'd followed the sound of some indie rock band into the workshop of Alexandra Drake. No more than an unlocked door separated the storefront from her work space. Was she really that trusting? Her back was to him and with the music pounding she couldn't have heard his approach.

Had he taken advantage of the perfect opportunity to check out her security system? Eyeball the safe sit- ting in the corner? He could have taken photos and she wouldn't have noticed.

No. He hadn't. He hadn't done any of the tasks a self- respecting thief would have accomplished in seconds.

His gaze had gone straight to the hips gyrating to the beat of the music, tightly clad in jeans, her legs not long, but shapely. She had small feet encased in boots. Above the swinging hips, her torso was still. She wore a navy tank top, not an ounce of extra flesh on her. Her bare arms revealed elegant swells of muscle. Her hair was black and wound into a big messy bun with what looked like chopsticks stuck through to hold it in place.

Her eyes were glued to a magnifier and he watched her hands. Those small, efficient hands. Using some kind of tool that looked like small pliers, she was twirling a strand of hot metal as though it were a piece of cooked spaghettini, draping it around a colored stone. He knew the moment she felt his presence. Those glorious hips slowed, her back stiffened.

Still, she finished the meticulous draping of the metal before setting the ring into a clamp. Then she raised her head and turned to him. Too fast for him to pretend he hadn't been watching her.

He couldn't have pretended anything, anyway. He was too stunned.

The woman was gorgeous. Cool gray eyes of a tilted almond shape that suggested there was Asian blood in her. Pale skin, full, sexy lips that begged to be painted red, but which she'd only touched with some kind of gloss.

He didn't have time for lust. He had a job to do.

And yet somehow he couldn't help himself. He'd come on to her. Enjoyed flustering her, finding an excuse to touch her.

And now, he was preparing to steal from her.

He had a bad feeling about this. A bad feeling that he was going to break every rule he lived by and get to know one of his marks. After the dust had settled, obviously, a few weeks from now when she'd have moved on and wouldn't think to connect a missing set of jewels with a visit from Charles Pendegraff.

He called himself every kind of fool as he made his preparations, but he knew he was going to be stupid.

As crazy as it was, he was going to see Lexy Drake again.

2

AT SIX, AMANDA PEEKED into Lexy's work space. "I've closed up. I'm heading out now."

Lexy glanced up and rubbed her tired eyes. "Good day?"

"Three engagement rings, a few pairs of earrings and about a hundred of those bracelets that were featured on *Party Girls of Manhattan*."

Lexy laughed. It was amazing how slavish people could be when they saw their favorite star wearing something distinctive on a television show. She only had a small number of mass-produced designs, but since one of the women on the newest semireality show had discovered her work, her designs—especially the ones that appeared on the show—were snapped up.

"*Party Girls* will do for you what *Sex and the City* did for Manolo Blahnik," Amanda prophesied.

"Fine with me."

Her assistant glanced around the crowded space. "You planning to work all night?"

She rubbed the back of her neck. "No. A little longer. I want to finish this ring set, then I'll take a break."

"What did that woman and her daughter bring you, by the way? You seemed pretty excited. You know, that stylish woman with the perfect gray hair and her thin, pretty daughter."

"Mrs. Grayson and her daughter—" What was the daughter's name? She recalled the emeralds and diamonds with vivid clarity; she'd never seen such a perfect set, but recalling the details of the owners was always trickier. She closed her eyes for a second. "Judith, that was the daughter's name."

Lexy was becoming accustomed to the whims of rich people, and she was the first in line to recommend redesigning antique jewels into settings that would breathe new life into them, but as she'd opened the faded blue velvet box she'd had to suppress the urge to argue mother and daughter out of their idea to have this set broken down and reset.

The gems themselves were exquisite. Emeralds were funny things. The larger they came the more flawed they were likely to be. A few occlusions were expected but when she'd studied these gems through her loupe, she'd been astonished at the near perfection. And the color. Dark, clear green that she'd rarely seen outside a museum.

The setting was antique, no question. Like any personal ornamentation, jewelry went through fashions. But every age had its classics and this set was one of the most inherently beautiful she'd ever seen. Delicate strands of gold held the emeralds and diamonds in place but didn't compete, so the green fire flashed from the necklace. "These are exquisite. Are you sure you want to reset them?" she'd finally asked.

Mother and daughter exchanged a quick look. "Oh, yes," Mrs. Grayson had answered. "The set's a gift to

Judith, and she wants a more modern look. We both love your work. We're excited to see what you could do with these. You are such an artist and with these emeralds, I believe Judith will be breathtaking when she wears the jewels at the diabetes fundraiser next month." She smiled at her daughter. "I'd planned to give them to her when she got married, but now that she's twenty-five, and unmarried, I'm going ahead. Why wait? They've been in the family forever, and they really don't suit my coloring."

Lexy suspected what the older woman really intended was to display some of the family wealth around her daughter's throat in an unsubtle hint to potential suitors.

"You know, these emeralds are quite rare, and I suspect the pieces are hundreds of years old. You will compromise their value as antiques."

"Oh, they've been in the family forever. It's time they had a new look."

Lexy had accepted the commission, of course. It wasn't her business to talk clients out of her services and as lovely as the current set was, she knew she'd likely never have an opportunity to work with emeralds like this again.

Opening the safe, she withdrew the box and showed the emeralds to Amanda, who said, "Wow." They both studied the sparkle of diamond and deep, gorgeous green.

Amanda touched the edge of the swirled gold setting. "I've never seen emeralds that color. They're so rich-looking."

"I know. The color's spectacular. I think it's because they are so old. They must have come out of South

America centuries ago. Mayan stones are considered the purest and best."

"How much do you think they're worth?"

"Hard to say. But with the almost perfect diamonds and the unusual color and clarity of those emeralds, I'm guessing around a million."

"A million dollars?" Amanda squeaked.

"Yeah."

So Lexy had at least a million bucks worth of emeralds in her safe and a free hand to design settings that would help an unmarried twenty-five-year-old attract a rich man. Might be a little old-fashioned, not to mention Machiavellian, but this was also by far her largest commission ever.

"Don't tell anyone about this, okay?"

She knew she could trust Amanda. They'd worked together for about eighteen months. In her early twenties, Amanda Sanford was tall and thin, had slightly more than the fashionable number of tattoos and piercings and a penchant for painted leggings and army boots. She was also great with customers and seemed happy in her work.

Lately she'd been letting Amanda help her with some of the simpler settings. When she was swamped, it was amazing how useful an extra pair of hands could be. Amanda also possessed an artistic eye and Lexy often sought out her assistant's opinion when she was unsure.

AFTER AMANDA LEFT, Lexy finished the ruby wedding set. On a whim, she called her customer and let them know. As she'd half suspected the woman was so excited she wanted to come right over and pick up the rings.

So, her workday ended with a nice fat check, a happy and excited customer and one more peek at the emeralds.

Then, realizing she was starving, she opened the barely visible door that led upstairs to her living space. It wasn't nearly as fancy as the downstairs since she'd put every cent of her savings and a good chunk of the bank's into her business. Her tools, the display cases, lighting, decor, everything had to be consistent with her jewelry designs. Which turned out to mean expensive.

Which in turn dictated that upstairs she had little more than a bed, the most minimal kitchen and a couple of chairs and a table she'd found at Goodwill.

Pouring herself a glass of cool water, she noticed the familiar throbbing tingle of a burn on her hand. She regarded the spot, red and shiny, and recalled the guy who'd come in earlier, burdened by too much name and too little conscience. Charles Pendegraff III. Jeez.

He had a fiancée, and was going around staring at other women's butts and kissing their booboos all better. She shook her head. She gave that marriage a couple of years, tops.

So long as the happy couple lasted long enough to pay for her ring designs, she reminded herself, it was none of her business. For all she knew, Mr. Pendegraff III and Penelope had one of those open relationships where fidelity wasn't part of the contract.

She didn't understand that kind of relationship; she was firmly determined that if she ever decided to get married, she'd be the kind of woman who went after her husband with a shotgun if he ever strayed.

And, since her dad was a New York cop who worried about his single daughter, and had taught her all about self-defense and marksmanship, she could shoot the lying, no-good cheater right through the heart. Or any other part of his anatomy she felt like blasting holes in. Whoever married her better understand that.

Her mother, who was half Chinese and very traditional, would probably come back from the dead to help her bury the corpse.

The image of Charles Pendegraff rose up before her and she felt her trigger finger squeeze.

Odd that she should have such a strong reaction to a stranger, but she knew that the biggest part of her disgust was the undeniable attraction she'd felt to the man. But then she already knew her taste in men wasn't nearly as flawless as her taste in jewels.

As she finished her water the phone rang.

She checked the call display and picked up. "Carl. Hi."

"What's up, Sexy Lexy?"

"Just got home from work."

"All tired out from the long commute?" he teased. Carl Wiesenstein was one of her tight group of friends, all of them artists or craftspeople. He was a metalsmith who was making an amazingly good living considering that his specialty was house numbers and door knockers. "Come out and celebrate. I sold a five-thousand-dollar door chime today."

She laughed. "You've got to love New York."

"Oh, baby, I do. I'm getting the gang together tonight at Emo's. Nat and Bruce are coming, Ella if she can get a babysitter, a few others. You in?"

The thought of a night out with friends was tempting. She'd been working way too hard lately. But she knew she wouldn't go. Not tonight. "I'm so sorry. I've got to work."

"You work too much."

"I know." For a second she was tempted to tell him about the emeralds resting in her safe, but Carl wasn't known for discretion and all she needed was for him to be overheard while he was telling her friends about her big day—as she knew he would. Maybe when she got million-dollar pieces sitting in her safe every day she'd become blasé, but for tonight she was worried that some burglar might overhear Carl and it was dead easy to find her studio. Even though her safe was supposed to be uncrackable, she really didn't want it tested.

"I've got a rush commission. You know how it is."

Carl chuckled. "Not feeling sorry for you. You'll charge them through the nose to turn around a design fast."

"Gotta love New York," she said again. Frugality might be fashionable, but not to her clientele.

"If you decide to get a life, we'll see you at Emo's later."

"You got it."

She almost changed her mind when she opened her fridge and found nothing in there but half of an old pizza and a corked bottle of wine she didn't even remember opening.

She tossed both and called down to a Thai place for delivery, then she kicked back, cranked the music up, pulled out her sketchbook and started playing with ideas for the emerald and diamond set.

At midnight, she turned out the light, but Lexy couldn't sleep. A restlessness possessed her. She knew it was excitement. She loved her muse, she really did, but the damn woman was a workaholic slave driver. Ideas were chasing each other through Lexy's mind faster and more confusing than a stock car race.

After a couple of hours of tossing and turning, unable

to turn off her brain, she flipped on the light, looked at the sketch pad on the floor and knew that she needed to see those emeralds again. Her latest idea was bold, almost crazy, but she thought the gems were so unusually brilliant that they could dominate a bolder setting than the one they'd rested in for half a millennium.

THE ENTRANCE TO Alexandra Drake Designs was an eye-catching blue. Bight, shiny, as close to neon as paint can get, but the dramatic look suited her storefront and was oddly in keeping with the neighborhood, a place of avant garde shoe designers, exclusive little nooks selling nothing but handmade Italian bags, lingerie boutiques.

The woman was crazy not to have a decent security system, but then Charlie doubted she'd ever had to store anything as valuable as the emeralds that he assumed were currently residing in her safe.

It was almost too easy.

Broome Street was as quiet as it ever got. He could hear his soft footfalls on the pavement. In his black slacks, turtleneck and shoes he could pass for a man taking a walk after a night at the theater perhaps, or a meal at a good restaurant. The March night air was cool, crisp, and when the wind picked up, that man could as easily melt into the shadows of a doorway. And unlock the far-too-simple mechanism on the lock of Alexandra Drake Designs. This was the kind of lock he'd started his career with as a teenager. It took him less than a minute to take care of the main lock. The dead bolts took little more than a minute.

As the door of Alexandra Drake Designs opened and he slipped inside, he wished she at least had an electronic security system, something to give him a bit of excitement.

Charlie ought to be grateful he could be in and out in only a few minutes, with the Isabella Emeralds, but he had his pride. He might be a retired thief, but he was still the best. A little challenge would be good; otherwise a man could become complacent, lose his edge.

Silent and dark as a shadow he made his swift way past the dark shapes of her display cases to the back, to the door that separated the storefront from the small workshop. He was frankly insulted to find the door wasn't even locked. How was a thief to remain on top of his game when his marks were so damn sloppy?

He felt his way around her table, where he'd watched her work earlier, grinning at the memory of her body rocking out while her hands created magic. He'd been shocked at the punch of lust that damn near flattened him when she turned and he received the full impact of her eyes. Eyes that ought to be in a porcelain doll instead staring at him from that strong-looking body.

He'd be back.

He'd give the woman time to get through the shock of the break-in. A couple of weeks, then he'd casually stroll in here, with Penelope conveniently history. He planned to ask the jewelry lady out.

In silence, he knelt before the safe.

At least the safe put up a fight.

For the first time since he'd stood outside in the night contemplating the pathetic excuse for a lock, he felt his peculiar set of skills being called on.

The safe was an older, German model and he respected it. As safes went it was stubborn, thick walled, heavy, fireproof, blastproof, tamperproof.

But not Charlie proof.

They never were.

He flexed his fingers a few times to limber them, crouched, slipping into the zone, the blissed-out state that told him he was doing what he was born to do, and went to work.

ONE OF THE MANY ADVANTAGES of a live/work loft was that Lexy didn't have to commute very far to her job. She didn't even have to dress. Shoving on a pair of jeans and a sweatshirt, she pulled on a pair of purple and pink slipper socks and made her way downstairs.

Excitement was bubbling and she knew her imagination was working on overdrive keeping her from sleep. She'd learned to live with the quirk. Her creativity kept her designs fresh and edgy, sometimes surprising even herself. So she lost the odd night's sleep. She'd live.

She loved her studio at night. There was a hush that was almost palpable. Even though the traffic noise never ceased, and sirens pierced the night silence regularly, there were no customers, no movement, no commerce.

She could set herself to design knowing no one would bother her.

The door to her living space connected to the back room of the shop. As she neared the door she stopped, certain she'd heard something.

What?

A tiny scrape of sound, possibly nothing at all, but she couldn't shake the feeling that someone was behind that door.

Probably it was nothing. The creak of an old building, some animal she'd rather not think about nosing around in the alley, but not only had she been raised by a cop, she'd watched too many horror films to open any door behind which ominous sounds could be heard.

Instead she retraced her steps silently, grabbing the gun from her bureau drawer and taking her cell phone from its charger.

Deep breath, and down she went again. Silently.

At the door, she paused and listened. Was that a scrape? A click?

She eased open the door and flipped on the light.

And her eyes widened in surprise.

Charles Pendegraff III was standing nonchalantly in front of her safe. Her wide-open safe. The same one that was supposed to be unbreachable. And in his gloved hands, he was holding Mrs. Grayson's emeralds.

For a second neither of them spoke or moved. Then he motioned to the gun in her hand and said, "At least you have some idea of security. Is it loaded?"

Not that she'd ever surprised a burglar before, but she'd have expected a little more drama. Maybe false protestations of innocence or an attempt to run. At least you'd think the man would replace the emeralds in the safe, but he did none of those things. Simply leaned against the safe like it was an open refrigerator and he was in search of olives for his martini.

"Not only is it loaded, but I am an excellent shot. Put your hands up, Mr. Pendegraff. Or whatever your real name is."

"Oh, it's Pendegraff all right." His eyes crinkled with sudden humor. "And this is a very interesting situation."

"It's not interesting. It's disgusting. You're stealing from me."

"Not you, technically. Look, let me explain."

She raised the gun so it pointed at his heart. "Don't move another inch."

Somebody started banging loudly at the front door of the store.

The noise startled her. She'd never had so much action after hours before. "Open up, police," a harsh voice yelled.

Pendegraff glanced at the phone in her hand. "You called the cops? I wish you hadn't."

"I didn't. They must have followed you."

His lazy and most puzzling amusement vanished. "You didn't call them?"

"No."

"Then, sweetheart, those are not the cops."

"You're a pretty lousy thief, aren't you? Both I and the police nab you?"

She started for the door that separated her work space from the front of the store, keeping her gun trained on him. "Put the emeralds back in the safe and let's go talk to the cops."

"Think," he said softly. "If you didn't call them, how would they have tracked me? You don't have a security alarm I could have tripped." She could have sworn he sounded petulant. "No security cameras. And I've been in here ten minutes. If they'd followed me, they'd have been in long before now."

"Maybe—" A crash had her turning her head. The cops had broken down her front door without giving her a chance to open it? That was pretty aggressive.

One second, Pendegraff was leaning so lazily against the safe you'd have thought he was napping, and the next second he was behind her, one hand grabbing her hard against him, the other wresting the gun from her grip.

She was no weakling and she fought to keep control

of the weapon, jabbing him with her elbow, stamping on his foot, but her sweater socks were useless and her assailant was stronger than he looked.

Crashing sounds continued out front, she was sure she heard breaking glass, and then her own gun was jabbing her in the back. "Scream and I'll shoot. Let's get out of here."

3

HE HAULED HER OUT THE SAME door she'd come from and dragged her up the stairs to her apartment. "Fire escape. Where is it?"

"I'm not telling you." She was furious with both of them. With him for the whole escapade and with her for losing control of the situation. Not to mention her gun.

"Trust me, those guys downstairs are a lot meaner than I am. We really don't want to run into them."

She heard another crash. Pendegraff ran to her window and peered out.

She flipped open her cell, tried to call 9-1-1 but he grabbed it out of her hand before she could complete the call, tossing the phone onto her bed.

He yanked up the window sash. "Out," he said, pushing her through the window and onto the fire escape, dropping out beside her. "I swear to God if you make a sound or do anything I don't like, I'll shoot you. Now climb down."

"I'm wearing socks," she told him in a furious undertone as the crisscrossed wrought-iron bit into the soles of her feet.

"Good. It'll keep you quiet. Now move!"

He stayed right beside her as she stepped down, surprisingly as quiet in his shoes as she was in her slipper socks.

The fire escape was in good shape, but it was rickety and creaked as they made their way down. Still, no one came to investigate. *Thanks a lot, New York's Finest,* she thought bitterly.

They hit the pavement below and she felt a stone bite through her socks.

"Run," he ordered, grabbing her arm and breaking into a sprint, giving her no choice but to follow.

They ran, but cobblestone streets weren't designed for a woman in slippers. He didn't seem to care, hauling her along at a fast pace. She prided herself on being in pretty good shape, but she could barely keep up with his long-legged sprint. If his goal was to keep her too breathless to yell for help, he was doing an excellent job. She prayed she wouldn't step on broken glass or a nail or something.

"Hey," a man's voice yelled.

"Don't turn around," Pendegraff warned her. "Move."

They pounded down toward Canal Street and she saw a black limo glide toward them. She waved the vehicle down, almost sobbing in relief as it stopped.

Pendegraff didn't flinch, but with a quick glance over his shoulder, he dragged her toward the car, opening the back door and shoving her inside. The limo was sailing away before he'd closed the door. She heard the click of the locks sliding smoothly into place even as she grabbed for the door.

"Nice timing, Healey," Pendegraff said.

The limo took the corner at a sedate glide, and as it did so she watched through the tinted glass as a thickset guy in a cheap tweed jacket ran into view, gun in hand. When he saw the car, he slipped his gun under the flap of his jacket, then pounded past them.

"A getaway limo?" she panted. "Are you kidding me?"

She banged her head back against the leather headrest, frustration surging through her.

"It's very convenient. In New York a limo is barely noticeable and the tinted windows provide excellent privacy."

"Great. You stole the emeralds out of my safe, have your own getaway limo. And what are you planning to do with me?"

The gaze he sent her was speculative. He seemed relaxed and very cool sitting back in the black leather seat. "I haven't completely decided yet."

"Well, when you do, could you let me in on the secret?" She ought to be frightened, she knew that, but somehow she couldn't seem to work up any true fear.

"It's been a stressful night. Why don't you join me in a nightcap?" He reached for the bar built into the back, which was conveniently set up, right down to the fresh ice in the ice bucket. Swanky.

"I have a better idea. Why don't you drop me off at the next corner and I'll grab a cab home."

"Scotch all right?"

She rolled her gaze. "Fine."

"Rocks or straight up?" he asked in that lazy tone that was beginning to set her teeth on edge. As though they were at the yacht club for a social engagement.

"Rocks."

The ice tinkled into the crystal tumbler. "I promise I will let you go, unharmed, but I can't do it quite yet." He passed her a glass. Raised his own in a silent toast. "I promise, you can trust me."

She snorted. "You robbed me. I don't normally trust guys who break into my safe and confiscate my jewels. Call me a cynic."

She sipped her drink. She wasn't a big scotch drinker but he was right—it had been a crazy night and between the break-in, the police raid and the kidnapping, her nerves were a little jumpy. Naturally it was some ancient whiskey that had no doubt been lovingly distilled by kilted magicians a century or so earlier. The drink was smooth and rich.

He leaned back, and she thought that if she hadn't caught him red-handed, she'd never have believed the elegant man beside her was a thief. The knife pleats were still sharp in his black trousers, his Italian loafers showed not so much as a smudge of dirt despite racing through the streets of SoHo, his black turtleneck rose and fell with slow, even breath, as the man casually sipped his drink.

"Does Penelope know you're a thief?"

"Penelope?" His dark eyebrows rose. "I have no secrets from Penelope."

"Is she a thief, too?"

"She's more…" He seemed to consider his words carefully, and once again she caught the familiar amusement lurking in his eyes. "Support staff."

"You must be a pretty successful thief if you can afford limos and Italian loafers." She stumbled over the final word as a wave of fatigue washed over her. She was more tired than she'd realized.

"How about you?" he asked. "Do you have a significant other? Husband, boyfriend?"

"Worried someone will come looking for me?" she asked. At least she tried to ask the question. The words formed in her head but it felt as if there was a wad of cotton stopping them from making it to her mouth. Her head began to swim and in that moment she realized that there was more than scotch in her glass.

She jerked her head to face him. "You bastard."

He reached out slowly, oh, so slowly it seemed, his arm snaking like a Dali image, all long and loopy, to take the glass from her hand. "You'll be fine. I promise."

She struggled to keep her wits about her, jabbed the window control. If she could get some fresh air, maybe she could fight whatever he'd used to drug her. But even as she flailed for the button, she could feel herself slipping from consciousness.

LEXY WOKE WITH A SENSE of disorientation, as though she were on vacation and waking in a strange bed. But as her eyes opened slowly, the horror of what had happened to her came rushing back. She'd been in the back of a limo, she'd drunk scotch—not more than a few sips—and then she'd passed out.

Her mouth felt dry, her eyes were heavy and scratchy, and her head ached. She raised a hand to her face, rubbed her eyes. Then she looked around.

There was a little natural light coming in through a shuttered window. Enough to show her the ghostly outlines of a bedroom. She was in bed. Not her own. And she was alone.

She threw back the covers. Discovered she was in the same clothes she'd been wearing when she was kidnapped. But someone had removed her slipper socks. She pushed her bare feet to the floor and got up. Whoa. A little wobbly. She waited for her legs to steady, then padded to the shutters and opened them.

Gray light pushed sullenly into the room. As she looked out, she saw snow and trees. Huge, dark green trees and plenty of them.

Snow?

Something told her she wasn't in Manhattan anymore. Her window was in an upper story of what looked like an architecturally interesting house, which sat in a snow-covered clearing in the middle of a forest. A single set of tire tracks led to a parked 4x4. If there were neighboring houses she didn't see them. All she saw were trees. Everywhere she looked, trees, a gray sky and it was eerily quiet. It felt as though this place had been stuck in the middle of nowhere. To a woman who'd spent most of her life in Manhattan, all these trees and isolation were a little freaky.

There was no sign of anyone around. She unlocked the window and hauled up the sash, half surprised to find it opened. But then what was she going to do? Jump? At the very least a two-story fall would leave her with broken bones. She stuck her head out the window, filling her lungs with cool, moist air. The house was gray cedar shingle, all sleek lines and modern angles. A satellite dish perched incongruously from the roof.

A large bird swooped low over the trees and a chipmunk chattered. Apart from pigeons and crows, she wasn't really good at identifying birds, but she thought this might be some kind of hawk. Some predator that pounced on innocent animals, those that were smaller and inoffensively going about their business. Rather like she had before Charles Pendegraff III had pounced on her.

Lexy didn't like being a victim. And she most certainly didn't like that she'd been spirited to heaven knew where, with a thief who'd stolen property out of her safe. Not only did she have Mrs. Grayson's commission to design, but she had several other projects on the go. No time for a kidnapping.

When she crossed to the door she discovered it opened as easily as the window. She closed it softly and retreated back into her room. She needed to think before confronting her kidnapper.

She also needed to brush her teeth. This place seemed pretty ritzy. The furniture in her room was simple pine, but it had the high-end country look of simple furniture that cost a fortune. The bed was big and comfy; a couple of large armchairs flanked a fireplace and a partly open door led to an en suite.

The room reminded her of a luxury ski resort. Expensive, comfortable and in the middle of nowhere.

The bathroom thankfully possessed not only a toothbrush still in its wrapper but a basket of toiletries and a stack of fluffy white towels. The tap water tasted fresh and clean so she filled one of the two glasses she found on the granite vanity and filled it, drank the contents down in a couple of gulps and refilled the glass.

Sipping her second glass of water more slowly, she took stock of her reflection, which was a mess. Her hair was all over the place, her makeup had smudged and her clothes—which were pretty casual to begin with—looked as though she'd slept in them.

She brushed her teeth, then took a long, hot shower, washing away the last of her drug-induced grogginess. A white bathrobe hung on the back of the door—reminding her more and more of an upscale hotel—so she slipped it on and opened the drawers and cupboards in the bathroom hoping for a comb or brush.

She found both. Also hairstyling products and a limited supply of essential cosmetics still in their packaging. Her first instinct was to refuse to make herself pretty for a kidnapper, but she soon threw that idea aside. She had her own confidence to think of and it was amazing what a little lip gloss and some mascara could do.

Blow-drying her hair, putting on a little makeup, these small tasks steadied her and gave her some sense of normality.

When she returned to the bedroom and checked out the closet and drawers, she was only mildly surprised to find clean T-shirts, pajamas, track pants, a hoodie, outside jackets, rain boots and blessedly unopened packages of underwear and socks. He either had a lot of unexpected guests, or the kidnapping business had a high turnover.

She dressed swiftly—the only thing of her own she wore was her jeans—and then, pushing her shoulders back and her chin up, she left the bedroom in search of her captor.

Her feet were soundless on the thick carpet that covered the floors. The upscale mountain retreat look continued in the hallway. A muted palette of taupes and grays on the walls and woodwork highlighted several paintings and drawings that were so good she suspected they were originals. Hot ones, no doubt.

At the bottom of the stairs, she hit a slate entrance hall and landing. She listened, but heard no sound coming from anywhere. A flutter of panic in her chest as she wondered if she'd been abandoned here, but then she remembered the 4x4 out front.

She went searching. And discovered that Mr. Pendegraff had exquisite taste. Everything was of the finest from the leather furniture in the living room to the liquor in the cabinet.

She found the kitchen at last, and found Charles Pendegraff III sitting in a deep chair in a den area off the kitchen sipping coffee and watching a plasma TV. He glanced up when she entered the room and immediately flicked off the television.

He'd changed yet again, she noted warily. From rich fop to black-clad jewel thief, now he looked like an upscale mountain man. He wore jeans, a chambray shirt and hiking boots.

"Good morning. Would you like some coffee?"

"Is it drugged?"

His eyes clouded. "No. And I'm sorry about that, by the way. I couldn't think of another way to handle things."

There wasn't any point in him drugging her now, she was pretty certain. And she was a weak, weak woman unable to resist the scent coming from the sleek coffeemaker. "All right, then."

He rose, went behind the granite breakfast bar and poured a dark stream of coffee into a blue pottery mug that was much too ordinary and cheerful to be part of this house.

"Milk?"

"Yes."

He opened the door of a stainless steel fridge that she saw was fully stocked, withdrew a carton and placed it on the black granite countertop beside the coffee mug. "Sugar's in the pot there," he said.

She took her time preparing her coffee exactly the way she liked it. She was determined to stay calm. The coffee was delicious. Strong and rich and she felt the caffeine punching up her energy. Good.

"What would you like to go with your coffee?" he asked, as though he was her waiter. "I've got eggs, breakfast muffins, some—"

"I'd like some answers."

"I know. And you'll get them. Over breakfast."

"I'm not hungry."

"You will be. You like omelets?"

Frustration enveloped her, and forgetting her vow to remain calm, she marched up to him, right behind the granite breakfast bar and into his space. She stalked up until there were only a couple of inches between their bodies. She was so close she could smell him, hints of sandalwood from his shower gel or shampoo or something, the fresh laundered smell of his shirt, the smell of thieving hot man underneath it all.

His green eyes were wary and he'd missed a spot when he shaved. All that her mind processed while her anger boiled.

She slammed her coffee mug down on the counter. "I don't want eggs. I want answers. Yesterday you came into my life, into my store, into my work space." She began to list his crimes on her fingers, from mildest to most venal. "You lied to me, you broke in after dark and stole from me." Her third finger hurt when she hit it to emphasize the third item on her list. "You kidnapped me." Bang she hit her fourth finger. "And you drugged me. Now I have no idea who you are or where I am and I want to know." Her fingers curled into a fist. Even though she wanted to punch him as hard as she could, she wasn't foolish enough to do it. Instead she rapped her closed fist against the other open palm. Smack, smack.

"And I want to know, now."

For a second he simply stood, gazing down at her. She wished she were over six feet tall so she wouldn't have to look up to meet his eyes. It was infuriating being shorter and slighter than her foe.

It took her a second to realize that he was looking at her, not in a kidnapper to victim way, but in a man to woman way that made her blood stir. What was wrong with her?

How could her body respond to a criminal?

Needing an excuse to back away from this far-too-close contact, she picked up her mug of coffee. A tiny crack had formed in the bottom where she'd smacked the pottery on the granite. She only wished it was Pendegraff's head she'd cracked.

And she stepped back.

"Okay," he said. "You want to talk first, we'll talk."

"You'll talk," she reminded him.

THE DEEP, COMFY CHAIRS in the den made her want to curl her feet beneath her. Under different circumstances she thought she'd like this place. Wherever it was. There were no newspapers conveniently lying around, no phone book sitting by a phone that might give her hints to her current location.

She sat up straight, her feet on the floor.

He refilled his mug and took the other chair. Sipped, slowly, in a way that suggested he was stalling for time. Her foot began to tap against the floor.

"I actually am Charles Pendegraff," he began.

"The third?" Skepticism tinged her tone.

A brief grin lit his face. "Yes, though I only mention the number when I want to come off as a pompous ass."

"You're good at it," she said sweetly.

"As you've obviously gathered, I'm a thief." He paused, shaking his head. "*Was* a thief. I'm retired." He glanced at her and his gaze darkened. "And, until last night, I'd never been caught. I must be losing my edge."

"Caught by me and the cops."

"Lexy, those weren't cops."

"Oh, come on. Why would I believe you?"

He reached for the remote control. "You're not going to like this. I recorded a news broadcast from New York this morning."

He flicked on the screen and pushed a couple of buttons. A newscast she knew well, one she often watched as she was getting ready in the morning, told her it was going to be cooler in Manhattan today, then there was the usual banter between the show's host and the meteorologist. Then the news.

"I'm really not sure what the U.N. funding crisis has to do with—"

He held up a finger. "Wait."

And then there was news footage of a block of buildings she knew intimately. It was her street.

"A suspicious fire broke out last night at a well-known jewelry designer's SoHo premises, destroying the store and the living space above it."

"A fire?" she whispered.

The film that went with the voice-over showed her street, the blackened front of her store, the pretty blue paint all bubbled and black, all the windows smashed and uniformed firefighters spraying water into her apartment.

"Emergency crews responded at 4:11 a.m. when a neighbor saw flames coming from the building that houses Alexandra Drake Designs. Ms. Drake's residence was above the studio."

Like a horror movie, she watched as a man rushed to the store's entrance and had to be forcibly restrained by the police officers standing out front.

"Carl," she cried softly.

Next thing, her friend was being interviewed, clearly distraught.

"Lexy's a good friend. We asked her to come out with us tonight, but she said she had to stay in and work. I was walking home and saw the fire truck." He glanced around frantically. "I can't find her. Did she get out okay?"

The camera cut back to the on-the-scene reporter. "Police and fire crews aren't saying much at this point, only that they will be investigating the cause of the fire, which they are calling 'suspicious' and that robbery is suspected."

The pictures of the fire crews at work continued to play as the morning news anchor took up the story. "Investigators recovered the body of a woman from the scene. It will be several days before a positive identification can be made of the victim, but at this hour, Alexandra Drake is still unaccounted for."

Then there was video playing of her at a gala, taken a few months ago, wearing one of her own necklaces. A jeweled collar. Talking about her work.

The host continued: "Alexandra Drake was a fast-rising young jewelry designer in New York. Her work appears in the collections of movie stars, royalty around the globe, and has been featured in a handful of recent movies. Her specialty was wedding and commitment rings." Close-up of Lexy at the gala, speaking. "I believe every love story is unique, so shouldn't your wedding ring be as personal?" Back to the host. "Alexandra Drake was twenty-eight years old. And in the meat packing district today, a suspicious package in a garbage bag turned out to be—" Pendegraff flipped off the TV.

"*Was?* They said was." Her shock must have shown on her face; she couldn't have stopped it.

The man beside her nodded. Looking grim.

"They said there was a dead woman in my place. Why would there be a dead body in my apartment?"

"I don't know, Lexy. We'll figure this out."

She rose. Unable to sit still one more second. "Yesterday my life was so normal. Exciting even. And today, my business and home are destroyed, I have no idea where I am."

She glared at her companion. "Oh, yeah, and I'm dead."

4

"YOU'RE NOT DEAD."

She rubbed her eyes. "Right. Just kidnapped." Rage filled her and she welcomed the fiery anger; it was so much easier to deal with than the despair she felt tugging at the edges of her consciousness. Everything she'd worked for, her home, her business, gone. "This is all your fault."

"I know you aren't ready to believe this, but I saved your life."

It was the last straw. "You stole from me."

"Technically I was reclaiming stolen property. Look, you've had a shock. Let me cook you some breakfast and we'll talk this through."

She barely heard him. "I have to call my father. He'll have seen the news. He'll think I'm—" She couldn't finish the sentence. Since her mom had passed away five years earlier, her father had become increasingly protective of her, encouraging her to come home and live in the Queens home she'd grown up in. She knew part of his problem was simple loneliness and his years as a cop had put him in contact with too many horror stories.

She couldn't allow him to believe she'd become one of them. "Where's the phone?"

Pendegraff put a restraining hand on her shoulder as she began searching for a phone. "Until I figure out who is behind this, who set me up and burned down your place, the safest thing you can do is stay missing."

"But—"

"It's for your own safety, Lexy. Your father wouldn't want you to put yourself at risk, would he?"

"You don't understand. He's a cop. He lost my mother to cancer…I'm all he's got left. He'll go to my place, he'll think it was me in that fire and he'll drive himself crazy. I have to get hold of him."

He rubbed her shoulder briefly before letting her go. "Give me half an hour to explain. Then, if you still want to, you can call your father."

She glared at him, at the flawed emerald eyes, the expensive tough-guy face. How could she trust him? He wouldn't even give out her location.

"Where am I?"

"I value my privacy. You already know too much about me. I really don't want you being able to summon cops to my door."

She remained silent.

"You're in the mountains. Still in the States."

"Not good enough."

Maybe he understood how helpless she felt and how much she needed a little information to help her cope. "Colorado. It's fairly remote, but the closest town is Aspen."

"How did I get here?"

"Private plane."

"Stolen?"

A slight grin cracked the serious expression on his face. "No. I bought it."

"So you're a pretty rich thief."

"I do okay."

"Where's the pilot?"

"You're looking at him."

Somehow, she wasn't surprised. "This is like one of those nightmares where you want to wake up, and can't."

"I'm truly sorry about your home and business. This is not the kind of stuff I get involved in."

"Right. You're a gentleman thief, I bet. Somebody Cary Grant would play in an old movie."

He smiled briefly. "Sit down while I cook you breakfast."

She picked up her coffee and followed him as he strolled to the fancy-schmancy kitchen, pulling down a gleaming steel frying pan with all the confidence of a top chef. She watched as he opened the fridge and began efficiently removing butter, brown eggs, spinach, cheese and some kind of fresh herb she wasn't enough of a cook to identify. She topped up her coffee and perched on one of the sleek kitchen stools.

"He cooks, he breaks into supposedly unbreakable safes, he flies his own plane. What other talents are you hiding, Mr. Pendegraff?"

He turned from his task and the glance he sent her was so full of sexual heat she felt as if her skin would scorch. For a second she couldn't breathe. "One day, I'll show you," he promised softly.

Instead of returning the icy glare he deserved, she felt a response so strong it shamed her. Heat rushed through her, making her light-headed. Well, maybe he was the sexiest man who'd ever kidnapped her, but there was one thing she was certain of: it would be a cold day in hell before she'd be getting naked with this guy.

"You've got thirty minutes to explain what the hell is going on. Start talking."

It was amazing how he could crack eggs, chop herbs, grate cheese and still manage to calmly explain a story that grew increasingly complicated as she listened. Her headache was gone and if she still felt a little fuzzy, she had no trouble following the plot.

"I help people retrieve things," he explained. "Quietly, without a fuss."

"You steal."

"It's a gray area. I used to steal, no question about it, but after a while the thrill wears off. Besides, I figured I should quit while I was ahead. Never caught."

"I caught you."

A flicker of annoyance crossed his face. So, that bothered him, did it? Good.

"Had you at gunpoint, too."

"I was unbelievably careless last night." He flicked a glance at her…a quicker, softer version of the sexual scorcher he'd lobbed her way earlier. "On too many levels."

He chopped whatever the herb that was with a vengeance. "And so were you."

"Me?"

"What are you doing with no proper security? Candy-ass locks and no video surveillance? Anybody can get in."

She shrugged. His words echoed her father's uncomfortably. How many times had her dad nagged her about security? "I figured I could take care of things. I live on the premises." She glared at him. "And the safe is supposed to be unbreakable."

"No such thing. Not to a guy like me."

"So what was a guy like you doing there? Spinning me some tale about wanting a wedding ring, then robbing me."

The knife stilled. "Can we clear one thing up? I wasn't robbing you. Had no intention of doing so. The only thing I took was the emeralds."

She snorted. "Oh, is that all? Do you have any idea what they're worth? My insurance would never cover that amount. I'd be ruined."

He shook his head. "You can't put a price on that set. What story did the woman give you? The one who brought in the emeralds?"

"How do you know it was a woman?"

"Please. I'm a professional. I didn't pick your place to knock it over. I followed the gems to your studio."

She drank coffee, stalling for time. She didn't want to give out any information, but if he'd followed the woman to her place he must know something about her. "She said she wanted them reset, modernized to give them to her daughter to wear. I got the feeling she was hoping to attract a rich husband by hanging a fortune around that girl's neck."

He glanced at her sharply. "The older woman did the talking?"

"Yes."

"Who did she say she was?"

"Florence Grayson."

He laughed aloud. "Oh, you've got to give the woman credit. She's got some guts."

"Are you saying that woman isn't Florence Grayson?"

"Nope. Technically I suppose they stole the gems from Florence Grayson. The young one? Pretending to be the daughter? She's Edward Grayson's mistress. Or was. I'm guessing Edward gave her the heave-ho and Tiffany treated herself to a little goodbye gift. The Isabella Emeralds." He poured eggs into the pan and breakfast began to sizzle.

"Wait, I'm getting confused. The mother isn't the mother, the daughter's the mistress—and what are the Isabella Emeralds?"

"I've met Florence Grayson. That wasn't her. I've also met the mistress, Tiffany Starr if you can believe that's the name she picked for herself. And as for the Isabella Emeralds, they're part of a legend. Should really be in a museum."

Lexy had an affinity for jewels the way some people have for water, or music. They all but spoke to her. She recalled the sadness she'd felt at the idea of resetting stones that were so perfectly at home in the delicate antique setting. "I thought they were some of the nicest and best set gems I'd ever seen. That deep color was so unusual. I'd only ever seen it in jewels that came from Mayan mines in Columbia centuries ago. I actually suggested they might want to rethink the idea of having the set redesigned."

"Your instincts were right on."

Something was tickling her memory. She closed her eyes for a moment. And then it came to her. She'd actually read about the Isabella Emeralds back when she'd been studying antique gems. "I thought the Isabella Emeralds had been lost."

"Nope."

"Weren't they rumored to have gone down with the *Titanic* or something?"

"I suspect the owner set about the rumor. Rich collectors can do some pretty strange things. They've been in a private collection, which pretty much means the same thing as lost to the world. Grayson is so terrified of losing those emeralds that he never lets Florence wear them. I didn't know he even owned the set until I was called in to recover them."

"Then how did the mistress hear about them?"

He threw an amused glance over his shoulder. "I'm guessing Mr. G got a nice charge out of decking his mistress in his precious gems—and nothing else, for his private pleasure."

"Historical gems as sex toys? Oh, please."

He chuckled. "You asked. I was giving my opinion."

"Is that what you'd do if you had them?"

He folded the omelet expertly in two. "If I had the right model." Something about his tone reminded her that the Isabella Emeralds were currently in his possession.

As was she.

"If I remember correctly, the Isabella Emeralds were a gift to Queen Isabella of Spain from Christopher Columbus, right?"

He nodded. Cut the omelet in half and slid the pieces onto two thick blue ceramic plates. "As part of a thank-you gift for funding his trip to America."

"In 1492."

"Exactly. Not only are the gems themselves amazing quality—"

"I noticed that. The diamonds are flawless, and the emeralds as close to perfect as you can get in that size. The gems alone would be worth a fortune, but their provenance makes them—"

"Priceless."

He slid a plate to the counter in front of her, handed her a knife and fork and a blue linen napkin.

"Thanks."

He brought his own meal and sat beside her at the breakfast bar. It was undoubtedly cozy and she might have felt uncomfortable if she weren't obsessed with the notion that she'd very nearly unwittingly destroyed a piece of history. "How could that woman have been so stupid? By getting me to reset the gems she'd be decimating their value and annihilating a piece of history."

"They'd be a lot easier to sell, though. You can't exactly put the Isabella Emeralds on auction at Christie's or post them on eBay and not have somebody notice."

"Wow. So where do you come in?" She dug into the omelet, found it thick and fluffy and full of flavor, which didn't even surprise her. She was beginning to think that Charles Pendegraff did everything well.

"Edward Grayson hired me to retrieve the gems after he discovered they were missing. Oh, he doesn't know he hired me. My chauffeur fronts for me at all client meetings. I prefer to keep my identity to myself. I go along electronically."

"Sneaky."

"I prefer the term *discreet.* Anyhow, Grayson asked me to get the set back, with no publicity, no police, no embarrassment. In return I pocketed a nice fee. Everybody's happy."

"Except this one went sideways. Publicity, police and a very embarrassingly dead body. Somebody screwed up. Great omelet by the way."

"Thank you. Somebody was set up."

"But why? It makes no sense. And who is the dead woman in my studio?"

He frowned. "I don't know for certain, but I could hazard a guess."

5

THE EGGS SUDDENLY FELT like cement as she swallowed and made the obvious connection. "You think the dead woman is Tiffany Starr?" She had met the woman, talked to her even. She hadn't reached her thirtieth birthday, and now she was dead? It was foolish and vindictive to steal priceless jewelry from a former lover, but did she have to die for her crime?

"Who else could it be? You and I were there when the goons started to break in. There was no one else in the studio or your apartment."

She shook her head. "No."

"So they threw in an already dead woman, torched the place. Days will go by before anyone realizes it's not you in there."

"Why? If what you say is true, why didn't Grayson stick to the plan? He'd have got his emeralds back and no one would ever have known she took them."

"That, Lexy, is something I'm planning to figure out."

He was looking at her with an intensity she didn't like. As though there were more bad news on the way.

"What?"

"My guess is that Tiffany Starr wasn't the only one who was supposed to die last night."

An unpleasant queasiness rolled through her. "You mean…?"

"You'd seen and handled the gems and I'd been hired to retrieve them. As I said, no one has set eyes on them since the early part of this century. I pegged Grayson as one of those fanatics who want to keep all their toys to themselves."

"Like a spoiled kid?"

"A spoiled kid with his own private staff of thugs and killers."

She sank her head into her hands. "I should have listened to my mom. I should have gone into nursing. Or teaching. Something uncomplicated, with a pension."

"Somehow I can't see you in an ordinary profession."

She groaned. "I know. It's my curse."

"Finish your eggs. It's always been my belief that you can't commit a crime on an empty stomach, and I'm almost positive you can't solve one, either."

She toyed with an orange slice but in truth she'd lost her appetite. As she played his words back, she dropped the orange. "Wait a minute. You said your chauffeur went into the meeting with Grayson instead of you. They think he is you. He's the one who's going to get killed."

"Don't worry about Healey. He can take care of himself."

She didn't know why she should be concerned about a man who'd aided and abetted her kidnapping, but then she was the sort of person who bought non-kill rodent traps and had, on occasion, transported a very angry rat to a new home.

Amanda had been horrified and flat-out refused even to open the door so she and the rat could get outside. Her breath caught in her chest. "Oh, my God. Amanda. She saw the women. I even showed her the emeralds." She jumped to her feet, her heart hammering painfully. "I have to warn Amanda." She ran past Pendegraff, headed for the door of the house. If the Jeep was still sitting there, she could get to a town, somehow she'd find a way back to New York.

She was out of the front door. Good, the Jeep was still there. Keys inside would be nice, but if not she knew how to hot-wire a car. Her dad had taught her a lot of useful skills over the years.

The gravel bit into her socks and the sun blasted her eyeballs but she barely noticed. Amanda was her employee, a friend, her responsibility. She had to warn her.

The Jeep was parked, a gray shape against the snow. She sprinted blindly toward it, was almost there when a strong hand grabbed her arm, almost pulling it out of its socket.

"Ow. Let me go."

"Lexy. Stop."

She turned to him, and in turning found herself bashing hard abs, a chest that felt like granite, looking up into a face that was surprisingly understanding. "I have to go. You've got to let me. Amanda trusts me. She's my employee, my responsibility." She panted, trying to get the words out and pull away from his grip at the same time.

"I know. It's okay. Healey's watching things."

"Healey? The guy who helped you drug and kidnap

me? Pardon me if I don't feel superconfident in his abilities to guard my friend."

"Healey's the most capable person I know. It's why I hired him."

"Those men are killers. You said so yourself. Killer trumps thief. You know? Like Rock, Paper, Scissors? Killer would trump them all. Crush rock, shred paper, smash scissors. This isn't a game. You've got to let me get back."

"I can't, Lexy. It's too dangerous. I'm trying to protect you."

"Then you have to let me call my dad," she said as calmly as she could. "He deserves to know I'm alive, and he can make sure Amanda gets police protection."

The understanding expression in his eyes hardened to stubborn. "Not possible."

"This is not negotiable."

A glint of humor softened the hard planes of his face. "Are you in a position to negotiate?"

At that moment all she knew was she had to protect her friend and she'd do whatever she had to. "I think so. I will do everything I can to get out of here, and I'm a pretty resourceful woman. You'll either have to tie me and lock me up, keep me drugged 24/7 or give me one phone call."

"We're in the mountains. Miles from Aspen. You don't even know what direction it's in."

"Like I said, I'm resourceful. Do you really want to keep chasing me down?" She was gambling, she knew, but a man who didn't lock her door, and who made such good omelets didn't strike her as a guy who was going to be happy dressing her in duct tape the entire time she was here.

"You're a pain in the ass, you know that?"

"I didn't ask to be here."

He squinted up at the sky as though the answer might be written there. Finally he said, "And if I give you that one phone call you'll cooperate?"

"I want to get the people who tried to kill me as much as you do."

"Come on." He turned on his heel and headed back for the house. For a moment she hesitated. She could have the Jeep going in less than five minutes without keys, thirty seconds with, but she didn't know the area, the roads, she had nothing with her, not a cell phone, money, not even shoes.

Reluctantly she turned and followed Pendegraff. Seemed one phone call was her only option.

For now.

The phone was, predictably she supposed, a satellite phone, so the call would be untraceable.

Before he handed it to her, he said, "How easy would it be for an outsider to connect you with your dad?"

"Not easy." She hadn't thought until this second that her father could be in danger because of her and the missing emeralds. She'd never been more thankful they had different names. "My great-grandfather changed his Polish surname, Dabrowski to Drake. He figured it would be easier for the kids to fit in. My dad was a Drake and so was I, but when I was a kid he went through some kind of Polish identity crisis and wanted to go back to his roots." She found herself smiling, amazed she could. "We took one memorable family holiday back to the old country, saw the town where his people came from, looked up a couple of cousins who didn't speak any more English than we spoke Polish."

"How old were you?"

"Fifteen, I think. It was pretty cool and my mom

made him take us to Paris as well, so I had a great time. After we got home he decided to change his name back to Dabrowski. He wanted us all to be Dabrowskis but my mother refused. She said I already had a name, and I wasn't getting another one until I got married. So, my Dad's Dabrowski and I'm Drake."

"Even so, you'd better warn him to keep his guard up. I'm guessing Grayson will stop at nothing to get these jewels back. We have to be smarter than they are. Call your dad at the station. If he's not there, don't leave a message. Keep calling back until you get him."

"Okay."

She placed the call; for some reason her fingers weren't quite steady. What if she was wrong? What if somehow Grayson, or whoever was behind this, had made the connection between her and her father? Even as the phone was ringing she began to panic.

"Dabrowski," the familiar tone barked, sounding clipped and somehow toneless.

Relief washed over her and the familiar voice was so comforting to hear that she wanted to crawl into his lap and make all the ugly stuff disappear. "Oh, thank God. Dad, it's me."

For a second there was total silence.

"Dad? It's me, Lexy."

"Jesus, Mary and Joseph, you're alive."

"Yeah. I had to call when I saw the news. I knew you'd be worried sick."

"I gotta sit down." She heard fumbling and then he was back. "Where the hell are you? Your place burned, it's trashed, I thought you were dead." He sounded aggressive and angry, but also like he had a bad cold. She knew he was fighting back tears and her own eyes filled.

"I'm so sorry you were worried." She wrapped her hand tighter around the phone as though it were her father's hand. "It's a long story, and I don't have a lot of time, but I'm all right. I need you to do something for me."

"I'll come and get you is what I'll do. You seen what happened to your place?"

"Yes. I saw the news. Please just listen. I think I might be in danger."

"Then you get your ass back here so I can protect you."

"It's not that simple. Dad, if the people who burned down my place and killed that woman figure out you're my father, you could be in danger, too."

"What the hell is going on? Who's they? What are you involved in?"

"I honestly don't know, but it involves some jewelry I was working on."

Pendegraff was making wind-it-up motions with his hand. "I don't have much time, but it's really important you not go to the media or do anything that would make a connection between us. And watch your back, okay? You're all I've got."

"It's not my back I'm worried about. Honey, I need you to come home."

"I can't. Not until I figure out what's going on. Is there any ID yet on the body?"

"Too soon. Everybody still thinks it's you. Once they rule you out, then we start trying to figure out who the Jane Doe is."

"I might be able to help. There's a woman named Tiffany Starr…no idea what her real name is. We think it might be her."

"How do you know that?"

"I'm sorry, Dad, I've got to go. I'll call you again soon."

"Wait. Who's we? Who are you with?"

"I can't tell you that, but I promise I'm safe. I'll call again as soon as I can. Don't worry."

She hung up before he could get started on the worried rant she could feel building.

He was so concerned for her that she doubted he'd think for a second about his own safety, despite her warning.

And what was the point of her being stuck out here in the middle of Colorado when people she cared about were in danger? "I have to go back to New York," she said.

"Oh, I agree."

"You do?"

"Yes."

"Oh, thank God. When can we leave?"

"Thursday."

"Thursday? Why, do you have a dental appointment?"

He sent her one of his "James Bond superspy everything's a secret and women adore me anyway" looks that were really starting to piss her off. "A social engagement."

She opened her mouth to protest but he continued, "And you're coming with me."

"I thought you said—"

"What size do you wear?" He looked her up and down like he was Vera Wang's personal assistant. "Four?"

And he'd have made a good one. "I buy my own clothes."

"Fine. I'll make sure there are plenty of choices. Now,

if you'll excuse me, I've got work to do." He turned away and took a step.

"You're going to rob your own house?" she asked sweetly.

He turned back. "I'm a legitimate business person now. Mostly."

"Wait. You can't leave me here with nothing to do."

"I've got books, satellite TV, make yourself at home."

"To make myself feel at home, I'd have to torch the place," she snapped.

"I know this is hard for you, but I am trying to figure this thing out."

"By watching your stock portfolio and planning parties?"

"Oh, this is a very special party. A charity gala event in Manhattan. The Diamond Ball. You wouldn't want to miss it."

Something about his tone had her narrowing her eyes, amazed at how stupid she'd been. "Grayson's going to be there, isn't he?"

"You bet your sweet ass he'll be there. Since he and his wife are hosting the party, he can hardly avoid showing up."

"It's too bad I don't have any of my own jewelry with me. I could display my wares in front of New York's glamour crowd."

"Never mind. I've got a very nice set of emeralds you can borrow for the evening."

She swallowed. "You're serious, aren't you?"

"Absolutely. If Grayson's as obsessed with those jewels as I think he is, he'll go crazy when he sees them on you. And in public."

"Won't he try to get them back?"

"Oh, I hope so. But he can't do anything in the middle of a social gathering with hundreds of very well connected guests, now can he?"

"I don't know. The guy probably killed his ex-mistress, he tried to kill you and me, destroyed my home and business. I really don't think he'd stop at much."

"When are you going to start trusting me?"

"Oh, let's see. Probably when you stop holding me against my will."

He took a step closer. There was a glint in his eyes that made her want to take a step back, but naturally she held her ground. She had her pride. "From now on, I'll try not to do anything against your will."

There he went again, with his annoying sexual innuendos, which were so corny she should be rolling her eyes. Except that when he gazed at her in a certain way and his voice took on that deeper timbre, she responded in some deep and utterly female part of her that didn't care all that much about kidnapping or inappropriate behavior or sexual innuendo. That was the part of her that lit up like a rocket when he got close.

Heaven help her if he ever stopped teasing and actually made a physical move on her.

Of course, she'd drop him like a stone. Gun-wielding wasn't her only self-defense tool.

At least, she thought she'd drop him like a stone, but she hoped she wasn't going to be tested since she had a teensy feeling that the one doing the dropping might be her. Right onto her back.

He was looking at her mouth, the way a man looks at a woman's mouth when he's thinking about kissing her.

Her own lips started to tingle in anticipation as he drew closer, even as her brain was clamoring at her to stop acting like a fool. What, did she have Stockholm syndrome after one day of captivity that she should be thinking of locking lips with her kidnapper?

While she was trying to think of all the reasons why she shouldn't kiss the guy—and there were plenty—the decision was taken out of her hands. His mouth closed over hers. He kissed her slowly, thoroughly, then he raised his head, rested his hands on the wall above her head.

"I've been wanting to do that since the moment I saw you."

She was so surprised she could barely believe what had happened. The man stole everything, even kisses.

"What about Penelope?"

He was still staring at her lips so his voice was a little vague as he said, "Penelope?"

"Your fiancée?" She was pretty sure he'd made Penelope up, but she needed every defense she could muster against a man she found dangerously attractive.

"Oh. Right. Penelope." He traced her lower lip with his thumb. "We broke up."

He kissed her again.

He wasn't the only one having trouble focusing. She could barely form words. "When? When did you break up with Penelope your fiancée?"

"Right after I met you."

He was such a liar. He nibbled her lower lip. Good kisser, though.

"How did she take it?"

"Like a champ. You have the most kissable mouth I've ever seen."

"Thank you." He placed another series of kisses on her lips, then tilted her chin so he could kiss his way down her neck. She'd never noticed how sensitive her skin was there.

"Sounds like she was glad to get rid of you."

He nipped her lightly when he reached her shoulder. "She was brokenhearted, naturally, but she understood that I could never marry her if I was obsessed with kissing you."

"That would be awkward." She put her arms around his neck, looked up at him through her lashes. "So, do I look like her at all?"

"No. Totally different."

"She's tall?"

"A little taller than you. Not much."

"And she's blonde?"

"Redhead. And what they say about the temper is true, by the way." He came back for one more kiss on her mouth. "But to give Penelope credit, she never pulled a gun on me."

She didn't like remembering how easily he'd wrested that gun away from her. She was going to have to seriously get back in shape when she got home, and rev-up the self-defense lessons.

He straightened. "That was definitely worth waiting for. But, much as I'd like to stay here and make out all day, I've got to get to work. My office is back there if you need me," he said, gesturing to a hallway running to the rear of the house. "Try to stay out of trouble."

As she watched him walk away she thought he was too late.

She licked her lips slowly; seemed she was already in trouble. Deep trouble.

6

HEALEY'S ELBOW WAS JAMMED into a tree branch; he was pretty sure he'd ripped out the knee in his black trousers and something was crawling on the exposed skin of his leg. Something that felt like an ant.

He didn't care too much about any of that. Or the way his body was unnaturally folded into one of the ornamental trees that lined the block, the young leaves filling out the branches. What he cared about was feeling like a pervert. Looking through a window at a hot chick undressing would be great if the girl knew you were looking and wanted you there. But that wasn't the case.

He was doing a job because Pendegraff told him to and that was how he got paid. But when he'd crawled up here to check that Alexandra Drake's assistant, Amanda, was home, he hadn't imagined she'd be undressing.

Or that the tree would be so perfectly reflected in her dressing-table mirror. If he squinted, he could make out a darker shadow within the rustling leaves that was his own bulk. So long as he stayed still, she'd never clue in that he was here. But if he moved, she'd make him instantly.

So, acutely embarrassed, he stayed.

Amanda Sanford. That was her name. The assistant in Alexandra Drake's jewelry studio. A pretty small fish, but if Charlie was right, the same goons who'd torched the jewelry studio might well come after the only person who might know where Lexy was.

Of course, she didn't know her boss was alive, never mind where she was. Hopefully the two women would be reunited if he could keep Amanda alive and Charlie could do the same for Lexy.

Amanda was changing her clothes, which wasn't good news on a whole bunch of levels. First, it meant she was going out when he'd hoped she'd stay tucked in safe and tight. Second, she was taking her sweet time about the changing part and hadn't even bothered to pull the blind. Any fool with a pair of eyes could watch her.

A diamond stud glinted in her nose and when she turned the light caught the ring in her eyebrow.

A black shirt came off first. Her skin was tawny, and she had a long, lean torso. Her bra was one of those why-even-bother affairs that do more to show off than to hide the assets in question.

He dropped his gaze with determination. He couldn't shirk his duty, but he could for damn sure look away instead of staring at her like a Peeping Tom.

Resolutely he let his gaze slide, unable to help himself from noticing the tattoo of a sailboat on her left shoulder blade. He'd seen tatts on girls before, usually running to flowers or birds, or those tough-girl barbed-wire rings around the bicep, but he'd never seen a sailboat.

She put her hands to her waistband to undo her jeans

and he forced himself to look even farther down. Her feet were bare. The jeans bagged at the bottom as she pulled them off, then stepped out of them.

And he thought she had the prettiest ankles and calves he'd ever seen. Ankles? What the hell was the matter with him? He didn't have a thing for ankles. Never even noticed them before.

She turned, walked a few steps and he noticed another tatt. This one on her ankle. An anchor. Again, an odd choice for a woman and definitely at odds with the sailboat on her shoulder. From his peripheral vision, he could see her body moving, reaching into a closet but he kept his focus firmly on her feet and lower legs.

To his enormous relief he watched her step into a dress and pull it up over her hips. Giving her time to get the top part on, he waited a moment before raising his gaze. Her dress was short and floated around her. Feminine.

She opened a narrow drawer in the dresser and stared down into it for a long time. Then she drew out a necklace. She touched it as though it were an heirloom, running her finger along the edges of a chunky-looking design of gold and some other metals. In the mirror he watched her face crumple and tears started to fall. He wished he could reach out and wipe them away, tell her her friend and employer wasn't dead at all but alive and safe.

Naturally he couldn't, so he watched as she carefully fastened the necklace around her neck, then swiped her hands over her face. She walked out of sight, and returned a few minutes later, her face looking freshly washed. Her bangs clung damply to her forehead.

Without the heavy makeup she appeared much

younger and vulnerable. Her eyes were shadowed by lack of sleep and, he suspected, shock and grief.

She'd lost both her employer and her job in a pretty dramatic fashion when the studio burned to the ground and a woman's body had been found in the building.

He watched as she pulled herself together, touching the necklace from time to time as she lined her eyes with black pencil, smudged some other stuff in a complicated arrangement and then laid on the mascara brush. She left her face plain and merely added a swipe of glossy lip stuff.

He watched as she sat on her bed and yanked on black stockings with big diamond-shaped holes, and then stuck her feet into tough-guy black boots.

He kind of liked the mix of softly feminine with kick-ass toughness. Wondered if her personality reflected her clothing style and wished he had the luxury of finding out.

At last she grabbed a bag with a chain that she slung over her shoulder, and left. He looked carefully around before lowering himself from the tree but the side street was momentarily deserted. As he hit the ground, he noticed that it wasn't, in fact, deserted. An elderly woman walking a tiny dog jumped when he landed on the ground a few feet away. He hadn't seen her before because an arrangement of branches had hidden her. Damn. She was eyeing him as though she were about to whack him with her purse.

He smiled. Held out his ring of keys. "Found 'em. My wife threw them out the window during a fight." He shook his head, shrugged. "I love her, but the woman has quite a temper."

"Take her some flowers," the woman advised.

Her dog, meanwhile, peed on the tree he'd just vacated.

After walking down the street in the opposite direction of the old woman and her dog, he turned left, circling around in time to catch Amanda coming out of her building. She had a cell phone glued to her ear and as she talked, he noticed that she touched her necklace a few times.

She dropped down into the subway. He followed from a distance, keeping track of her whereabouts without getting too close and at the same time trying to figure out if anybody else was tailing her.

He didn't think so. But he wasn't taking any chances.

AFTER TOURING THE ENTIRE mountain retreat Lexy knew that there were four bedrooms, a nice workout room downstairs, a wine cellar and a media room, and that Pendegraff wore reading glasses when he worked and was vain enough to slip them off when she barged into his office to find him typing on a sleek laptop, ignoring a stunning view of the mountains behind him.

"I need boots," she informed him.

He blinked as though adjusting to looking at her after focusing on his computer screen. He then glanced down at her slipper-socked feet. "Why?"

"Because I need to get some air. I'm going stir-crazy." She'd been obsessively checking the news stations for any update on the fire and its aftermath. But, apart from feeling gratified to discover she'd rated a small mention on CNN, she didn't get much for her trouble but more depressing footage of her destroyed property. It was beyond strange to see her neighbors, a couple of fellow designers and even the star of the reality show, *Party Girls of Manhattan,* talking about how talented she was and how much they loved her and her jewelry.

"She was like her designs," a smarmy no-talent rival said into the camera. "One of a kind, and she'll never be replaced."

Lexy wanted to throw something. She stood up and shook her fist at the stupid TV. "I'm not dead," she yelled at the screen. That was when she knew she had to get some exercise.

Charlie seemed less than excited about the idea of her leaving the house but she'd had enough of being a victim. "I'm going out. There must be some kind of trail or something."

"I'll come with you," he said.

"No. I need to be alone. I don't want a jailor."

"But—"

She put her hands on her hips and glared. "Look, buster. You want me to trust you, which is a pretty tall order considering what you've put me through, how about you trust me. I said I'll come back, I will."

He nodded slowly. "What size are your feet?"

"Six."

"I've got some women's boots that are a seven. Best I can do. Wear an extra pair of socks."

"Ladies' shoes. Really. Can they be Penelope's?"

"My mother's."

She turned away. "Whatever."

"You'll find them in the mudroom closet."

As he'd promised, she did find a few pairs of shoes, hiking boots and snow boots. All sevens. The hiking boots fit okay when she tightened the laces. Pendegraff came into the mudroom as she was preparing to leave. He carried a white parka and a pair of ski gloves. He helped her into the coat, handed her the gloves, opened the door for her and stepped outside behind her.

This door opened to the back of the house, but the view was similar to that at the front. There was snow everywhere she looked, white and, except for some random animal tracks, untouched. And where the clearing ended, there were trees. Massive evergreens that marched toward the towering mountain peaks.

"You want some snowshoes."

"I do?" She was doubtful, never having been on a pair.

"Yeah. It's easy. Just walk normally. You'll get the hang of it."

He disappeared back into the mudroom and returned with snowshoes. Metal ovals that he strapped onto her boots for her.

"Thanks," she said reluctantly. She didn't want him to be thoughtful, any more than she wanted to be disturbed by his proximity, or find that his kiss was still imprinted on her mouth.

He extended his hand across the clearing to a gap in the trees. "That's the main trail. Stay on it and you'll be fine. Turn around when you get tired."

"Where does it go?"

He pointed to the summit of a mountain. "Take you a couple of days to get there, but on a sunny day, it's a great view."

She headed off without a backward glance, knowing he was watching her. Presumably to ensure she didn't sneak around to the front of the house and steal the 4x4.

Snowshoeing was a lot like normal walking, so long as she took her time. She practiced in the clearing until she had the hang of it and then attempted the trail. It was pretty rough with snow-covered rocks ready to trip the unwary. But the air was so clear and it smelled pure and heavenly when she filled her lungs. The trail headed upward meandering only slightly so she was soon puffing.

Oddly enough, as she got higher things started to fall into perspective. She wasn't dead; she was very much alive. And in the middle of an adventure the likes of which she'd never imagined.

She was also tough, resourceful and creative. Anybody who messed with her better be prepared for that.

A hawk circled in the sky, and a gray and white bird she didn't recognize landed on a tree and watched her, cocking its head as though wondering what on earth she was doing lumbering along on plastic and metal dishes.

By the time she'd stomped back into the mudroom a couple of hours had passed and she was starting to move beyond shock to "now what?"

"Hi, honey, I'm home," she yelled.

Pendegraff came out of his office. Took one look at her and grinned. If he was relieved she hadn't tried to steal the Jeep and take off, he was obviously trying to be cool. "You've got rosy cheeks."

"Had a great workout. Thanks."

He nodded. "Coffee's fresh. Help yourself." And he went back to his office.

She poured coffee and then checked the news stations again. Nothing new.

Went downstairs and made use of Pendegraff's very nice home gym, then showered and changed into a comfy pair of sweats and a T-shirt with a pink snow-flake embroidered on the front of it.

Not her usual look, but kidnappees, she reminded herself, can't be choosers.

7

AMANDA HOPPED ONTO a crowded subway car heading downtown and Healey squeezed himself in at the opposite end of the same car.

He was getting tired of following this restless woman around. She'd been to an avant garde art gallery for a couple of hours, gone shopping without buying anything, stopped for a coffee and stared sightlessly out the window. He wished she'd just go home and give them both a rest.

She got out near Third and Lexington. At first he thought she was going in to one of the Indian restaurants scenting the air and reminding him he hadn't eaten in a while. A black and white cat nestled in the doorway of a corner market regarded him with lazy interest.

They passed an Asian fusion place and then she joined a short lineup of people heading into a bar.

He studied the menu outside the Asian place feeling his hunger increase as he contemplated the possibilities.

She was in. He waited. When she emerged, he'd follow her home and make sure she got in safely. But what

if Grayson's people somehow got her in the bar? He
stared at the neon sign. Emo's. After an hour when she
hadn't reappeared, he couldn't stop worrying about her.
He entered the bar.

He was twenty-nine years old and walking into the
bar made him feel ancient. The clientele was young and
definitely tended to the alternative. In his jacket and
dark pants he stuck out like a Wall Street banker at a
folk festival.

Nothing he could do about it now, so he headed for
the end of the long bar and checked the place out. It was
pretty busy. Lots of Goth types, some college students,
artsy folk. There were half-moon shaped booths along
one wall and then mingling space, which was pretty
crowded. Amanda sat at a booth with a group of friends.
All had drinks in front of them but they didn't look like
they were partying it up. He recognized the young guy
who'd been on the TV looking for Lexy the night of the
fire.

A couple of the women were wearing distinctive
jewelry pieces, similar to that worn by Amanda. They
kept touching their necklaces, or bracelets, or earrings
as they talked, occasionally laughed. A digital camera
appeared and was passed around, causing more laughter
and a few tears. He had to believe this was a modern
wake.

When it was Amanda's turn with the digital camera, he watched her expressions shift between fondness,
amusement and grief. A grief so fresh it hurt him to
look at her. Suddenly she passed the camera to the guy
beside her, as though she couldn't bear to see the photos
anymore. She looked up, his way, and before he could
turn, their gazes connected.

Damn. He hadn't meant to make eye contact. Didn't

want connection between them. So he looked away, but
not before recognizing the raw pain in those eyes and
once more wishing he could ease it. Her eyes were blue.
Bright, piercing blue under the tousle of short black hair.
On a normal night, he'd go up to her. Say "hi." But this
wasn't a social outing. It was work.

He turned away and took a pull of his beer.

A moment later he felt her beside him. As crowded
as the bar was, and as full of women, he knew it was
her without turning his head. Her presence was like a
scent he couldn't ignore or get out of his mind.

"Hi," she said, her voice kind of rough, like a
smoker's.

He turned to her. Saw that close-up her eyes were
even prettier than he'd thought. Blue and dew-drenched,
like flowers in the rain. "Hi." This was bad. So bad.
He wasn't supposed to talk to her; he was supposed to
be invisible. He absolutely wasn't to think about those
contradictory tattoos, to wonder how that sailboat would
taste under his tongue, to remember the lacy bra and the
swells of flesh beneath it.

Nice going, Healey.

She leaned a slender arm on the bar and he realized
she was a little the worse for wear. The diamond stud
flashed. "I'm Amanda."

"Healey."

"I'm a little drunk."

"Sorry to hear that."

She giggled. "You shouldn't be. I'm so bad when I'm
drunk."

He swallowed, hard. He could blow her off, should
blow her off, but then she'd go hit on some other guy and
that seemed an incredibly stupid and dangerous idea.
She didn't know she could trust Healey, but he did.

"You seem kind of sad," he said.

"Buy me a drink and I'll tell you all my troubles."

Giving in to the inevitable, he motioned to the bartender. "Jaegar Bomb," she said. "We're sort of having a wake. You should have one, too."

He nodded and the bartender went to prepare the drinks.

"I can't sit there anymore. It's too depressing." She grabbed his upper arm, as though for balance. "Life is short, you know? I never realized how short it is. What's the point of dreaming about the future or worrying? You have to get out there and live it. Every day. Every minute. Every second." She laughed, a deep, sexy sound. "And definitely, every night."

The bombs came at that moment. She picked up the shot glass, popped it in the glass of Red Bull. And downed it. A drip of liquid ended up on her lower lip and he had to restrain himself from licking it off her.

She shook her head. "Wow." She laughed up at him. "Now, you."

He threw the drink back. The bitter and sweet mixing in his mouth. Which was pretty much how he felt about this woman coming on to him. He wanted her and knew this was the last thing he should be doing.

But then his usefulness as a tail was now completely blown, so he figured staying close to her was one way to protect her. And besides so far he'd seen no evidence that anyone was following her or watching her movements, except him.

"So, how come you're the only guy here in a suit?"

"Just got off work. Thought I'd come by and grab a quick beer and some food. What's good here?" He suspected that some food in her stomach would be a good plan.

"Nachos are pretty good. The burgers are okay."

He ordered nachos and a burger and she said, "So, what do you do where you have to wear a suit and work late?"

"I drive a limo. You?"

"I'm, ah, kind of unemployed right now." She didn't regale him with the dramatic tale of how her workplace had burned to the ground along with her employer, which he thought showed a lot of class.

"Taking some time?"

"Yeah. I'm not sure what I'll do next. I can't waste my time anymore, you know? Life's too short."

"So you said."

"Well, it is. There was a time, maybe last week, when I'd have noticed you, seen you checking me out and figured if you came to talk to me, great. If you didn't no biggie." She grabbed a nacho, piled it with sour cream and salsa, "Not anymore. What if you didn't come talk to me? I'd have missed an opportunity." She said the word *opportunity* very carefully. "I'm not doing that anymore. If I like the look of someone, I'm going to talk to them. Anything wrong with that?" She shoved the loaded chip in her mouth.

"Not a thing." But this oddly protective instinct he had about her kicked in. "You probably want to keep it in a public place until you're sure, though."

Her eyes lost their shadow of sadness as speculation took their place. "Are you telling me that you're dangerous, Healey?" Her voice took on a sultry edge. The filmy, floaty dress brushed his thigh as she moved closer. Her hand followed, rubbing up and down. "Is that why you want to keep this in a public place?"

Impossible not to feel aroused by her words and the blatant invitation of her hand on his thigh.

Her hand was moving, closing in on her target. He couldn't think what to do, so he grabbed her hand in his and said, "Let's get out of here."

He thought her friends would protest but they were deep in discussion and he doubted they'd even noticed. He led her out onto the street. It was dark, with pools of light spilling from the restaurant windows. The first shadowed patch they hit, she pushed herself against him, shoving him against a brick wall and pressing her body to his. She lifted her face, kissing him blindly.

He understood that she was seeking oblivion from her pain, even as he knew he should stop her. But the minute their mouths met, he was as lost as she.

He didn't have the excuse of alcohol or grief; all he had was this strange sense of connection, and lust as strong as anything he'd ever known.

Her hands grabbed his shoulders, ran down his back. Her body was lean and quick moving as she rubbed herself against him.

He pulled away. "Let's get you home, wildcat."

She giggled. "Thought you wanted to do it in public."

"Nope. What I want to do to you needs a lot of privacy."

"Yeah?" The word came out in a breathless rush. "What do you want to do to me?"

"I'll tell you on the subway. Come on." It occurred to him that she'd be a lot safer at his place than her own if anybody was looking for her.

As he kissed her, he smiled inwardly. Charlie had had to forcibly abduct Lexy to get her to go to his place. Amanda, on the other hand, was eager to get to Healey's place. Score one for him.

8

AMANDA WAS BURNING UP. There was something about this guy with his dreamy artist's eyes in the hard face that compelled her. Maybe because he was like one of Lexy's designs, all contrasts that went together in a delicious package, she couldn't resist him.

Impulsive, that was what she was being. And so what? She couldn't stand the heavy weight of grief anymore. She needed a couple of hours off. Maybe some hot sex with a stranger would kill the pain for a bit, since the drinks hadn't helped at all. In fact, if she let herself, she knew she'd become maudlin and start to cry. And the way she felt right now, she'd never be able to stop.

Lexy had been her friend as well as her boss. She'd started as a basic retail clerk but in the months they'd worked together she'd become a lot more. She ordered supplies, took care of the window displays and some-times—those very special times—Lexy let her help, asked her advice.

Amanda had been an art student when she'd applied for the job. It was originally a co-op placement, but she and Lexy had hit it off and the jewelry designer ended up hiring her. She'd been able to shuffle classes and work until she'd finished her program. Since then she hadn't done much in the way of art. She wasn't even sure what medium she preferred. She'd been happy working at the studio, helping Lexy with some of the simple tasks, hanging out with friends, being a young, carefree New Yorker.

Now she'd lost her job, her boss, her sense of the world as a normal place. She felt jumpy and vulnerable. If that awful, awful thing could happen to Lexy, anything was possible.

Maybe it was weird for Lexy's friends to go drinking the night after she'd died, but it was as if they had no rules or procedures to follow. None of them had ever been through anything so terrible. The bar provided the comfort of familiarity, they could share their stories, and maybe a few drinks would deaden the pain.

Hadn't worked, though. The drinks had only dulled the ache and left her with this burning need to do something wild. Sex was the most creative, life-affirming activity she knew. The second she saw Healey eyeing her, she knew she had to have him.

The subway had that eerie light that always seemed more bizarre at night. The people in their car—a couple of teenagers, tired people who looked like they worked shifts—were completely uninterested in the fact that she and Healey couldn't keep their hands off each other.

"My place?" she whispered against his lips.

"Mine." He kissed her, deep, until she felt weak with desire. "It's close."

She didn't care. She'd have done it right here if he'd asked her. "You said you'd tell me what you were going to do to me—you said you'd tell me on the subway ride."

"Did I?" He let his fingers toy with the hem of her dress, tracing the inside of her knee, finding the bump ridiculously exotic. "I'd rather show than tell. I think you have the sexiest knees I've ever felt," he informed her.

He traced a little higher, enjoying the landscape of bumpy stocking and satiny skin. The stockings looked like hell in his opinion, but they felt like sex.

They piled out of the subway, walked the few short blocks to his apartment, stopping frequently to push up against buildings in the dark and feel each other's bodies, tease each other.

He felt so good, surprisingly buff. His muscles were hard; work-out-three-times-a-day hard. The only other man she'd ever known like that had been a personal trainer she dated for a while. She loved the feel of his shoulders, his belly and chest when they rubbed against hers. The jutting evidence that he was into this as much as she was. But when she tried to slip her hands beneath his jacket, he stopped her, urging her on.

It felt as though they'd been teasing each other for hours; she was so hot she felt as if it must show.

Her dress brushing her thighs excited her, the size and solidity of the man beside her excited her, the scent of spring in the air aroused her and, most of all, the thrill of knowing she had no idea where they were going, where they'd make love, what his place would be like, what he would be like.

She was desperate enough that she didn't even care. He could lie on his back and think about the Knicks for all she cared. So long as he hung on to his impressive erection, she could do everything required to make sure they both had a good time. You could never tell with big, solid men.

He lived in a nondescript walk-up. No doorman. His apartment was on the second floor. She had a sense that the place would be full of workout equipment, a big-screen TV would dominate and his kitchen would be well-stocked with protein powder.

She couldn't have been more wrong.

He opened the door and flicked on a light, giving his place a visual sweep as though checking to make sure it was clean, which was what she'd have done. Except that this was the cleanest, neatest home she'd ever seen. Where was the junk? The dirty dishes? The clothes tossed in corners?

"I'll be right back," he said and disappeared through the doorway she assumed was the bedroom. She walked in. Usually she'd use these few moments to do some superficial snooping. What books were on his shelves? Did he have a collection of DVDs? Art on the walls? Trophies? Photos of old girlfriends?

But there wasn't much around that was snoop-worthy. One slim, sleek black bookcase held a few thrillers, some science books, a couple of volumes on natural healing. If he had family or old-girlfriend pictures they were hidden away somewhere.

She stepped into the kitchen, thinking maybe there'd at least be a few dirty dishes in the sink to make her feel more at home. Nothing. The sink was shiny.

"You want something to drink?" His voice startled her; she hadn't heard him return.

"Your sink is shiny." He must have a very good maid.

"I like to keep things neat." Finicky. Just great.

He came up behind her and wrapped his arms around her waist, running his lips up her nape so she shivered. "You want to stand here admiring my sink or get naked?"

Of course, maybe a man who shined his sink to perfection did everything to perfection. Maybe he wasn't finicky. But thorough. In the bedroom, she thought, thorough was very, very good. She sighed, leaned back into his warmth. "Get naked."

"I'm sure we'll get to the kitchen," he said, his voice low and sexy, "but for the first time, would you mind if we do it in the bedroom? I have this fantasy involving you and a mirror."

His voice was slow and heavy, like a drug in her ear, giving her a delicious shiver of excitement.

"You do?"

"Mmm-hmm. Come on," and he took her hand and led her into his bedroom. Predictably it was neater than a hotel room. The space was dominated by a low, European-looking bed with a simple gray comforter. Where a double closet had once been, he'd replaced it with a bank of drawers and one slim wardrobe cupboard. The mirror was a full-length one on the wall. She imagined him checking to see that all his buttons were done up correctly and that his socks were the regulation height as he dressed. A smallish flat-screen TV wall-mounted and a couple of Japanese block prints made up his art collection. Aside from the bed, the only furniture was a chair shaped like an *S*.

She considered going to check out the block prints since she liked art in all its forms, then he licked her shoulder and she decided she had plenty of time to check out his etchings. Later.

She turned, wrapped her arms around his neck and kissed him. Slow and deep. They'd been toying with each other now for what seemed like hours. She wanted the craziness to continue, to block out her pain, so she pushed her tongue boldly into his mouth, rubbed herself against him like a very passionate, sexually frustrated cat. "Why don't you tell me about this fantasy of yours?"

"You're standing in front of the mirror, undressing."

"Where are you?"

"I'm watching." He swallowed.

"From the bed? The chair?"

He shook his head. "I'm outside. I'm a stranger, watching you through the window."

"Peeping Tom. That's nice."

"You take your time undressing. You're kind of flirty about it."

"I'm doing a striptease for myself?"

Once again he shook his head. "You know I'm there, watching. You pretend you don't, but I can see the excitement in your eyes, the anticipation. I've been watching you, night after night, going crazy wanting you and you've been toying with me." His fingers tracked over her shoulder and his voice was so husky she felt as though the words were true. As though he'd been watching and wanting her for days. It was a good fantasy, one she could absolutely enjoy playing out, so she turned away, faced the mirror, wishing she was wearing more clothing.

She heard him settle into the chair—glad he wasn't going to go all method on her and climb out the window. She ignored him. Concentrating on her own reflection. Wow, she looked feverish. Her eyes overbright, her cheeks flushed, her breathing light and rapid. She felt a heat burning low in her belly and knew she wouldn't be able to drag this thing out very long.

For she knew that in teasing him she was tormenting herself and tonight of all nights she wanted release. Needed it with a fierce desperation.

She contemplated herself in the mirror; she had kind of a Twiggy-meets-Fight-Club look going on. No idea what she'd been thinking. Her hands went slowly to the neck of the dress. She thought her breasts were among her prettiest features so it only made sense to give him a hint of them and make him wait while she revealed the rest of herself to him.

This wasn't the first time she'd bedded a virtual stranger, but she'd quit one-night stands after college. She knew that it was grief making her act so foolishly but she was driven by forces she barely understood and certainly couldn't control.

There was a rush she'd all but forgotten in seducing a stranger, and with this game they were playing there was an extra level of sizzle in her blood.

Slowly she undid one of the buttons at her throat. A second button. The third revealed a hint of cleavage and the edge of a lacy black bra. The man behind her remained still but she felt his eyes on her reflection, was almost certain she heard a quiet "yes" as she began to reveal herself.

Taking her time about it, she lifted the hem of the dress and peeled it slowly over her head. She felt the burning intensity of his gaze as the fabric rose higher and higher until she'd pulled it over her head. He might be a neat freak but she wasn't. She tossed the dress into a corner, enjoying the way the crumpled dress stuck out in the neat room like graffiti on a white wall.

Boots next, she decided, bending slowly to untie them, giving him a good view of her rear and of her breasts straining against the lace of her cups. One by one she removed her boots, sending them sailing across the room with twin thunks.

The stockings were next. With infinite patience she peeled them down her legs, feeling his impatience burn in a way that only ignited her own and yet perversely made her slow her movements, torturing them both.

She straightened again and regarded herself in the mirror, knowing he was watching the same refection. Did he like what he was seeing? Her breasts weren't showgirl size, but they were shapely and held their own. Her hips were narrow, her legs long and lean. Not exactly a centerfold, but she liked her body, enjoyed sharing it.

She put her hands to her back to unsnap her bra and as she did so she glanced behind her. She was only checking to make sure he was paying attention, but as she looked at him their gazes connected and she felt as though lightning had struck. Heat, fire, sizzle, shock, she couldn't look away. Neither, it seemed, could he. So, while her body was displayed for him in the mirror, he gazed into her eyes. The snap gave, she eased the fabric away, and still he stared into her eyes. It probably wasn't the most intimate act of her life, but it sure felt like it.

The game ended.

He rose from the chair, fully dressed while she wore only a black lace thong.

He pulled her to him wordlessly, crushing her lips with his mouth, his hands going everywhere at once. She dragged at his shirt, his belt, bumped into his hands trying to perform the same tasks. If her striptease had been a thing of slow seduction, his was one of clumsy haste.

She almost growled in frustration as she fumbled at his belt until he pushed her hands away and did the job himself, though not all that suavely. He jammed his slacks down his legs, kicking them off in a way she knew had to be totally out of character. His briefs followed; his shirt was over his head and sailing into the corner to join her discarded clothing.

Pushing back the coverlet on the bed, he tripped her back so she fell into the soft, cool sheets. He followed, his body so hot against hers. His hands were everywhere, molding her, learning her. She felt soft and pliable compared to his boot-camp-tough body. And yet his mouth was so soft, tender almost as it traced her collarbone, her breasts. He licked the underside and she felt like screaming. The sensations were racing too fast for her to keep up. He reached down, slipping his hand into her panties, reaching for her center where she knew she was already slick with desire.

Suddenly he flipped her so she was on her tummy. His tongue traced the outlines of her tattoo. "Why a sailboat?" he asked in that gruff, deep voice that resonated with banked passion.

"To remind me I'm always free to sail away."

He continued rubbing her hot spot even as his mouth toyed with the tattoo and his lips traced the bones and ridges of her back.

He paused to remove her panties, sliding them slowly down her legs.

Then he was back, teasing her once more. "And the anchor?"

What anchor? She could barely think clearly with his hand moving in rhythmic circles. "Anchor?"

"The tattoo on your ankle," he said as though realizing she couldn't think straight.

"To keep me grounded," she panted.

He reached over and she heard a drawer open, then the familiar rustle and tear of a condom wrapper.

Heat rushed through her. Soon he'd be inside her, and she didn't think she could wait another second.

Sure enough she felt him nudge between her thighs, heavy and warm, finding the hot, open place. He entered her slowly, stretching and reaching, up, up to that magic spot. When he hit it she groaned.

He kept up the motion of his fingers working her clit and began to drive into her.

Wild, crazy sounds spilled out of her mouth, non-sense words and cries, as she bucked against him, driving them both to the edge of madness.

He took her up and over the edge and then as her cries subsided, he grabbed her hips and pumped, long, deep strokes that drove her up again until they both fell off the edge of the world. She sailed, and the weight of his body kept her grounded.

9

LEXY'S STOMACH REMINDED HER that it was dinnertime. Pendegraff's stomach must be on the same schedule for he'd emerged into the kitchen and was peering into the well-stocked fridge.

"Does someone shop for you or did you carry me unconscious into the grocer's to get all these supplies?"

He turned, and she noticed he'd showered also. And changed into a dark blue cashmere sweater and black pants. She thought that dark green would have looked better with his eyes, and wondered if he didn't wear dark green for that very reason. "Much as I like the mental image, I've got a housekeeper who cleans the place and shops when I let her know I'm coming."

"Handy."

"Grilled chicken okay? Or there's tofu. I wasn't sure what you eat."

"Chicken's fine." She washed her hands. "What can I do?"

"Salad?"

"Sure."

From the fridge he drew out a bottle of white wine

and, without asking her, opened it and poured two glasses.

"I feel like we should have a toast," she said. "I mean, this is probably the strangest situation I've ever been in."

He held his glass aloft. "Here's to the pleasure of meeting you. I only wish I had you here alone under different circumstances."

Their gazes connected along with their glasses. She didn't say what she was thinking, which was that she wished she had her own wardrobe with her if she was going to be alone with him. The pink snowflake put her at a disadvantage.

While he prepared the chicken, she dug through cupboards and found one of those gourmet packages of fancy rice and seasonings and put that on to cook. Then she put together a salad.

It was oddly homey making dinner with an attractive man. And completely strange at the same time. She thought he felt it, too, for they ended up having typical first-date conversation. Books they liked, movies they'd seen, music, sports, even New York politics.

When the dinner was almost ready, he said, "Okay with you if we eat in the den?"

"Yes, sure."

He had little fold-out tables, kind of like the TV trays her folks used to use only way fancier. Brought the food out and he flipped the switch to bring the gas fire to light. Normally she'd have been disappointed not to have a real wood fire, but right now she thought gas flames that could be controlled with a switch were just fine.

She'd wondered if they'd end up watching TV with their dinner but the screen stayed blank. Instead he turned his chair so he was facing her. "I've got the makings of a plan to catch Grayson," he said.

"That's very good news."

"I'm glad you think so, because the plan involves you." He glanced over at her. "How quickly could you make a piece of jewelry?"

"Depends what it is."

"Let's say I wanted you to copy the Isabella Emeralds."

She shook her head immediately. "Can't be done. There's no way I could source emeralds of that quality and color. You wouldn't have to be a jeweler to spot the fake. Grayson, or anyone who knew the piece, would see that the color was off. And while I can re-create the setting, getting the gold to exactly the right patina would take a lot of trial and error."

He nodded. Ate a bite of chicken. He'd put some kind of a rub on it and grilled it to perfection, naturally. "What if you wore the original to the gala? And the copy only had to fool somebody who believed they were getting the original? And only for a little while?"

"Bait and switch?"

"Exactly. In fact, this might work out better. Maybe we leave a trail of bread crumbs, make it easy for Grayson to get the necklace back, but we want Grayson to know he's ended up with a fake."

She blew out a breath. "If I had all my tools and an operating workshop, and all the supplies, and Amanda to help me, I guess I could have it done in time for the gala." Mentally she went through the steps and the time each would take, but of course in her imagination, she was working in her own space. "But I don't have my tools, or my studio and Amanda thinks I'm dead."

"None of those are insurmountable obstacles," he said in a voice of reason that made her want to hit him.

"Well, I could come back from the dead pretty easily, I've got friends who would lend me their studios and tools, but what I don't seem to have is the raw materials or the substantial wad of cash I'd need to buy them."

He turned to her and grinned. "See, I told you it was easy. You solved all the problems but one. And I can buy the raw materials." There was a light shining in his eyes that she thought was excitement. It was like he couldn't wait to waltz into Grayson's gala escorting her and a million-dollar heirloom he'd stolen. "We're a great team."

Instead of answering, she rolled her eyes.

"But I really don't want you back in New York yet. Somebody could spot you, or one of your friends could accidentally let slip that you were alive and well and working on a secret commission."

She opened her mouth to tell him that her friends were completely loyal. Then she closed it again. They were loyal, every one of them, but did she really want to burden them with her presence? Especially if someone was out to kill her?

"So you don't want me to copy the necklace."

"I do. I've got a…connection with a jeweler here, in Colorado. We've done some work together in the past."

She didn't want to speculate aloud on what relationship a thief and a jeweler might have that was mutually beneficial, since she was pretty sure he wouldn't tell her anyway. In truth, she didn't want to know. Having watched footage of her burned and ruined business over and over again, and hearing people talk about her as though she were dead, had given her a burning desire to bring Grayson to justice. If she had to work with people who operated in a murkier area, legally, than she, she guessed she was going to get on with it.

"I see. And does this jeweler have a full work-shop?"

"Yes."

She considered the feat he'd proposed to her. Copying someone else's masterpiece felt like forgery to her. Like trying to rip off the Mona Lisa. The emerald and diamond set had been created by a master of the day. But there was also something exciting about trying to re-create the artistry, using her own methods. No one who knew the original intimately would be fooled for long, but could she copy the original well enough to fool the casual eye?

"I wonder if we'd be better with synthetic emeralds," she found herself saying aloud.

"Lexy, if it's the money—"

"No. It's the color. Synthetic emeralds are often darker. Obviously a jeweler would know right away that the stones were man-made, but if we're going for visual illusion, then I might be able to pull it off." Her mind was spinning over possibilities. "I'll need real diamonds, though."

"Absolutely."

She glanced at him curiously. "Will you get them back?" Was it worth it to him to invest a fortune on getting revenge?

"I hope so. But it's not the most important issue." He seemed to hear her unspoken question. "I do not like being cheated, and I sure as hell don't like having people trying to kill me. Grayson pissed me off. If it costs some money to bring the guy down, so be it."

"Pretty high moral ground for somebody who made

their money from stealing things that didn't belong to them."

He rose, went to the fridge for the wine bottle and topped their glasses. "Oh, come on. You think Wall Street's not full of crooks? Name a profession that's never been touched by scandal. Law? Medicine? The clergy? At least I was an honest crook. I only stole from people who could afford to lose things."

"Did you need the money?"

He returned the bottle to the fridge and sat back down before answering.

"What kind of question is that?"

"A direct one. Sounds to me like you already come from a wealthy family, probably have a fat trust fund. I'm just asking whether you needed to steal to support yourself."

"Not technically." He picked up the pepper grinder and cranked it, adding spice to chicken that was already perfectly spiced.

"Okay, I'm curious. Why did you go into the larceny business?"

He seemed to realize there was nowhere he could go to get away from this conversation and that she wasn't going to give up. He shot her an irritated glance. "I didn't want to go into law, politics, finance or any of the other professions that were considered suitable." He shrugged and gave a wry grin. "It's the sad plight of the poor little rich boy. He can never be better than his father or whatever ancient relative amassed the fortune in the first place. I didn't want to follow…I wanted to set my own path."

"Really."

"I probably would have bummed around for a while and ended up toeing the line eventually, but luckily, when I was alone in the house one weekend, a guy broke in and tried to steal mother's jewels." He grinned in memory. "He was good, too. He'd have got away clean if I hadn't come home late and on my way up to bed heard something. Not even much of a noise, just one of those sounds that don't belong, you know? So you stop and take notice."

It was exactly like when she'd heard Charlie cracking her safe. The sounds hadn't been loud, simply out of the ordinary. She nodded.

"Anyhow, I snuck into my parents' room and he had the safe open and my mother's jewelry laid out on the bed, all nice and neat, like he was shopping. Naturally, being nineteen and thinking I was one tough dude, I tackled him."

He laughed. "The guy was pretty surprised. But he didn't seem like my idea of a thief. He was intelligent, well-spoken. If you'd passed him in the street you'd have pegged him for a university prof or a scientist or something, never a thief. Well, long story short, I agreed not to call the cops if he'd teach me everything he knew. We were partners for four years before he retired. Then I worked alone for a few years and now I mostly steal things back for people. Ironic, isn't it?"

"Oh, it's ironic all right. Especially as I'm the one who ended up homeless and dead."

"Well, bringing you back to life in the middle of the Diamond Ball, and wearing the necklace that supposedly got you killed, should go a long way to making up for that. As for the studio, I'm sorry it happened. Truly sorry. Did you have insurance?"

"Yes, but that's not the point. Of course I can rebuild, but it's going to take time and will really mess with my schedule."

"Right."

She rubbed her forehead with her hand. "But there's no point whining is there? Okay, I'll make a list of what I'll need. Maybe Amanda can contact my suppliers and get the gems."

"No. My jeweler can source what he doesn't have in stock."

She snorted. "Please yourself. But I guarantee you'll pay too much."

"Understood."

"How soon can you get Amanda here?"

"Tomorrow. I'll get Healey to put her on a commercial flight to Aspen."

He walked over and put a hand on her shoulder. "We'll get them, Lexy. I promise. We'll get them."

She nodded, looking up. His face was serious and yet she felt the excitement in him. He could tell her all the stories he wanted about being a rebellious teen, and maybe part of that was the truth, but the real reason he'd become a thief, and still continued to operate in the shadows, was that he was hooked on the thrill.

She caught a hint of his excitement and felt her fingertips tingle. She was going to forge a masterpiece starting tomorrow. She found she could hardly wait to get started.

Their gazes locked and she felt her breath hitch. She'd been absurdly drawn to this man from the first moment she saw him, knew he felt it, too, but she wasn't thinking clearly enough right now to be embarking on an affair.

Then his hand turned, rubbing her shoulder, moving slowly upward to cup her cheek. Abruptly he dropped the hand. "I'd better get back to work. Watch whatever you want on TV. Or there's some movies and stuff. I'll see you in the morning."

She watched him go, a slightly smug smile pulling at her mouth. She knew why he'd bolted. He wanted her, and he knew he couldn't have her.

Damn straight, he couldn't. Not yet, anyway.

Of course, she suddenly had all this sexual energy coursing through her body. She supposed she might as well make use of it and get to work herself figuring out how she was going to replicate the Isabella Emeralds.

"Hey," she called him back. "I'm going to work tonight, too. I'll need to study that necklace."

"I'll bring it to you."

"And I'll need that jewelry studio to myself. I don't want interference."

"You're not much of a team player, are you?"

"No. I work alone. It's how I like things."

"I also work alone. I guess the next few days, trying to work together and trust each other, should be interesting."

"Honey, you and I are never going to be a team."

He chuckled. "That sounded very much like a challenge. I have a weakness for challenges." He turned and went to get her the emeralds. Maybe he thought he was out of hearing range, but she heard him mutter, "And gorgeous smart-mouthed jewelers."

10

"YOU PICK UP STRANGE MEN in bars very often?" Healey asked Amanda over breakfast the next day, a bowl of healthy grains—far more than she could eat, with fresh bananas and frozen blueberries sprinkled on top and a healthy dollop of white stuff that she doubted very much was whipped cream. If she had to eat yogurt she liked it flavored with a lot of fruit. Somehow she thought Healey would disapprove. And she'd better not even mention that she was more a bagel and cream cheese and a quick coffee kind of gal.

She really didn't feel like getting a critique on her lifestyle so early in the morning, but his tone didn't sound judgmental, more genuinely curious. She pushed away the cereal and picked up her coffee. At least he had coffee. For a horrible moment she'd feared green tea.

"No. Not really. I was kind of crazy last night, you know? I really, really needed to get my mind off my problems and find an outlet."

A rare grin lit his face. "I'll be your outlet anytime."

He reached past her and pulled a bottle of disgusting

green stuff from the fridge that he said was full of spirulina. Which she was pretty certain was a kind of moss.

He drank right out of the bottle. "You want some?" he asked after he'd taken a few gulps.

She shuddered. "No, thanks." His refrigerator featured things like tofu and wheat grass. Organic fruits and vegetables, free-range eggs. No junk food.

"What happened to the guy who ordered a hamburger in the bar?" she asked in frustration.

He kissed her shoulder, leaving a green spirulina smudge. "I order the odd hamburger to impress girls like you. Plus, I crave them once in a while."

"We are total opposites. I crave healthy food once in a while. But mostly I live on the tasty stuff."

At least he had coffee. Free-trade organic blah, blah, blah that needed to be ground in small quantities and put into a French press, but the result was almost worth the effort, she thought, when she got up to make another pot.

"Want some coffee?"

"You drink too much caffeine. It's why you're so jittery," he commented.

"I'm not jittery. I'm in junk food withdrawal."

She dug a spoonful of yogurt and berries from the bowl and ate it, trying not to screw up her face at the sour burst of yogurt. She put down the spoon.

"Someone close to me died. Well, we were all close to her, those people I was with last night? It was sort of a wake. We were all immersed in grief and sharing our stories and pictures and suddenly I couldn't stand it anymore. I didn't want sympathy, I didn't want friends. I wanted sweaty sex with a stranger."

He was looking at her almost as though he understood.

"I wanted to disappear for a while. Have you ever wanted to be invisible?"

He chuckled, like he was having a private joke. "Frequently."

They chatted for a while until she'd made a respectable dent in her breakfast and finished her coffee.

"Well," she said, "I guess I should be going." She never knew how to exit gracefully from a one-nighter. Did she leave her number? Ask for his? Play it cool and say nothing? How did anybody have a night of intimacy and passion of the kind they'd shared and not want to see each other again?

He looked at her almost as though he was wondering the same thing. "What are you up to today?"

She shrugged. "I should probably start looking for a job."

"Or you could hang around for a couple of days."

"Don't you have to work?"

"I've got a pretty flexible schedule." He rubbed a hand along her shoulder, above the sailboat. "I'd like to spend some time with you."

And like that, her burden lifted a little. After Lexy's death she'd felt so unbelievably alone. Now, even for a short time, she had somebody who cared what she did all day. Who wanted her.

"Okay. Yeah. Sure."

It was only for sex, but right now? Sex was about all she had to give.

"So, what do you want to do today?"

She was hovering between responses. Did she most want to go shopping for junk food? Because if she was staying here she couldn't survive on nuts and berries, or did she want to take him to see some art that would blow his mind—or did she just want to drag him back to bed? She hadn't remotely made up her mind when his phone rang.

He checked the display and excused himself to the bedroom to take the call.

Her stomach did a weird dippy thing. Secret calls could only mean other women in his life. Not that she, a one-night hookup, was in any position to complain, but she'd felt like he maybe wanted to start something with her. Who'd said anything about it being exclusive?

She heard him arguing. And then he came out, holding the phone.

"Look," she said, "if my being here is messing anything up for you…I can leave."

He shook his head. "It's not that." He sank down heavily on the chair beside hers and took her hand. He looked so serious he was starting to freak her out. "I want you to know that last night was…amazing. And I wouldn't have changed a thing. You need to believe that."

"Okay." What the hell was he getting at? It was over? He had a girlfriend? Sure, she got it. Why not show her the door and be done with it? This hand-holding thing was a little strange.

And he still had his phone open.

"I'm a big girl, Healey."

"Okay. I know. There's someone on the phone who wants to talk to you."

He said into the phone, "Put her on."

She threw her hands in the air and backed away. "Oh, no. I'm not talking to her. You got woman trouble, you deal with it on your own. Don't get me involved." She looked around for her purse. "It was a hookup. We had fun. I'm out of here."

"Amanda, it's not what you think."

"Sure, okay, whatever." Where were her shoes?

"Amanda, stop. It's Alexandra Drake on the phone."

The air went out of her lungs and she felt the room sway. "What?"

"Lexy. It's Lexy on the phone. She wants to talk to you."

"Lexy's dead," she replied. And how the hell did he know about Lexy? She was sure she'd never mentioned the woman's name.

"No. She's not."

"I don't know what's going on, but I've got to get out of here. This is too weird."

He grabbed her arm, not hard, but firmly enough to get her attention. "Please, just take the phone."

He held it up but she shook her head. "Amanda?" The voice came faint and familiar. "Amanda?"

She grabbed the phone and plastered it to her ear. "Lexy? Oh, my God, is it really you? You're alive?"

"Yes. Alive and unhurt. I'm so sorry I couldn't call before. I'm fine."

"But…" She put her other hand to her head and collapsed on the couch before she fainted. "I don't even know what to ask first. I… We had a wake."

"You had a wake? For me?"

"Yeah." She laughed shakily. "Me and Carl and well, you know, the usual bunch. We met at Emo's and had a wake for you. Last night." She wiped her cheek, not realizing she was crying until the back of her hand came away wet. "And I thought about you and how I should have stayed that night and helped you. I... What happened?"

"It's kind of a long story. And I'm going to tell you everything, but I can't tell you on the phone. Look, I really need your help. I'm in Colorado. I need—"

"Colorado?"

"I know it sounds crazy. But I need you to come here and help me with a project."

"In Colorado?"

"Yes. Today. Healey, the guy with the phone, he'll get you a ticket. You've met Healey, right?"

"Oh, yes. We've met."

"Good, so—"

"Wait a minute. Why didn't you call me on my cell?"

"It's not secure. Amanda, criminals burned down my place and I'm pretty sure they murdered a woman. We need to stay safe. Healey's there to protect you."

"Huh, is that what he was doing?" She glared at Healey, who was standing across the room, watching her.

"I know this is a shock."

"How do I even know you're really Lexy?" she snapped.

"Don't you recognize my voice?"

"Not enough. Tell me something about me that no one knows."

"You've got a sailboat tattooed on your back."

She thought of Healey tracing the pattern with his tongue. Yeah, that was a real secret. "Something else."

"Um, your middle name is Jocelyn and you never tell anyone that. Ah, you're allergic to pistachios, when your mom threatened to throw you out of the house if you got your nose pierced, you got your nose pierced.

Oh, and you got the ring in your eyebrow when a drummer called Stephan broke up with you and went back to Frankfurt."

"Amsterdam." But that was exactly the kind of mistake a friend would make.

"Really? I thought it was Frankfurt. Okay, I remember his band was called Bionic Piss."

Amanda snorted with laughter. "What was I thinking?"

A familiar giggle echoed back. "I have no idea. So, did I pass the test?"

She glanced at Healey. Right now she trusted nothing that he was involved with. "Not so fast. I have some questions for you. What's your father's name?"

"Jed Dabrowski."

"Name the last commission you refused."

"Easy. Two weeks ago. The skull and crossbones wedding rings. So banal."

"What's your favorite sexual position?"

"Amanda, I'm not alone."

"You put me through hell, Lexy." The pain was still there. Weird. She wanted to believe Lexy was okay but on some level couldn't. "Besides, anybody could find out all that other stuff. This is more personal."

"I am never going drinking with you again."

Amanda was feeling better and better. She still remembered the night she and Lexy had gone for a drink after a late night at work. Somebody had left behind a sex manual and the two of them had looked through it and discussed favorite positions. Laughed at some of the names. "Quit stalling."

"Could you leave the room for a second?" she heard Lexy ask someone. "Hell, no," was the amused male reply.

A long suffering sigh whistled in her ear. "This is the last question I'm answering. The Lyons Stagecoach."

But she wasn't done punishing Lexy yet. The woman should have called her much sooner. "Man on top or woman on top?"

"It's a woman-on-top position," Lexy said, sounding as though she was speaking through gritted teeth.

Even though she'd pretty much accepted that the woman on the phone was Alexandra Drake it was still a huge relief to have the confirmation. "'Kay. I guess you really are Lexy."

"So, will you come to Colorado?"

"Sure." She gave Healey the evil eye. "It's not like I have anything better to do."

She gave the phone back to Healey, who spoke briefly to God knew who and then clicked off.

He came to her and tried to take her hand. She shook him off. "Don't even bother," she warned him.

"But you have to let me explain. I should never have slept with you."

She snorted. "That's my line."

"Amanda, please, let me explain."

"Fool me once, shame on you. Fool me twice, shame on me. You won't make a fool of me again. Clear?"

Reluctantly he nodded. "I never meant to hurt you."

She forced herself to sound casual. "Hey, you got me through a rough night. Gave me a few orgasms. I needed the release. You did your job, kept an eye on me. Now you need to get me to Colorado."

11

ASPEN CHARMED LEXY the moment she saw it. The town was quaint, European feeling, but you couldn't forget this was a ski destination. A glance up showed the wide, white ski runs like open hands, white fingers pointing to the collection of ski lodges, shops and restaurants in the village.

The drive to town from Charlie's house took fifteen minutes. Once the Jeep had powered over the unpaved private road, they hit a well-marked, well-trafficked area. Had she hot-wired the Jeep she'd have made it to civilization in minutes. "You lied to me," she said, incensed as the town came into view.

"No, I didn't. I told you the closest town was Aspen."

"You didn't say it was on your doorstep."

"You assumed you were in the middle of nowhere. I let you believe it. That's all."

Incredibly soon he was parking on a snow-covered road. A line of brick-faced buildings that looked like old warehouses contained a string of stores. Pottery, clothes, ski equipment and, surprise, surprise. Three jewelry stores. He took her into one of them where a young woman in jeans and a sweater asked if she could help them.

"Marcus is expecting me," Charlie said.

She nodded. Pressed a button under the counter. "You can go on back."

He led her through a back door and up a flight of stairs.

He knocked on the locked steel door at the top of the stairs and after a minute, during which Lexy felt herself to be under scrutiny, the door opened. "Charles, my friend," an older man with a beard and tiny round glasses said, shaking his hand.

"Good to see you, Marcus. This is the woman I was telling you about."

Marcus shook her hand. Not asking her name or seeming perturbed that Charlie hadn't introduced her. "Come in. I think I've got everything you requested."

He led them to a jeweler's workbench and handed her a loupe. From a locked drawer he withdrew several black cloth bags and a velvet-lined tray. He shook out diamonds from one, true emeralds from a second and synthetic emeralds from a third.

"Excellent," she said, as the raw materials she'd need tumbled out and caught the light. He'd followed her instructions exactly. She began to study the diamonds and found them of reasonable quality and the cut was right. It was the emeralds, however, which dominated the set and she was excited at the assortment she could choose from.

She glanced around a well-equipped workshop. "Ah, you've got the Black Max, excellent." The chemical, when applied with steel wool, would give the new gold an ancient patina. It wouldn't fool a professional, but she reminded herself, it wouldn't have to.

Marcus removed a heavy wool coat from a tree stand and eased himself into it. "I'm taking a couple of days off. Please make yourself at home. Charles knows how to contact me if you need anything."

Charlie leaned down to speak quietly into her ear. "Have you got everything?"

"Yes. I'll be fine."

"Okay. Don't let anybody in until I return." He gestured to the security camera in the corner that showed the stairs and landing. "I'll be back with Amanda in a couple of hours."

"Good. Excellent."

She barely waited for the door to close behind Marcus and Charlie before drawing out the Isabella Emeralds from her bag.

She opened the case and carefully took the necklace out and placed it on a velvet tray. She'd studied it at length the night before, making extensive notes and she thought she had a pretty good idea of how to duplicate the piece.

She pulled a second item out of her bag, the iPod she'd borrowed from Charlie. His playlist wasn't entirely to her taste, but by skipping the classical, the podcasts and anything remotely resembling folk, she had pretty good background sound.

She rubbed her hands together, stretched and flexed her fingers as though getting ready to play a piano concerto, and then she got to work.

Two hours later, Amanda arrived.

They screamed like young girls, hugged and rocked and laughed. "I am so glad to see you," she exclaimed.

"Not as glad as I am to see you!"

"Wow," Amanda said, looking at the work in progress. "I've never seen you copy anything before."

"No. It's not exactly my style. But I think I've figured out how to copy the necklace."

"Cool. Oh, Charlie said to tell you he's getting sandwiches. I told him you like ham and cheese and egg salad and you hate mustard."

"You are an assistant in a million."

Five minutes later, Charlie showed up with a paper sack containing sandwiches, coffee and a couple of bottles of water. Then he left and they munched sandwiches and drank coffee while Lexy filled Amanda in on everything that had happened.

Her eyes fairly bugged out when she heard the story. "I can't believe it. Were you scared?"

"Yeah. I was at first, but mostly I was angry, you know? And for some reason Charlie never really frightened me." She shrugged.

"It's 'cause he's so good-looking," Amanda said around a bite of egg salad. "In the movies they always cast good-looking actors as the heroes and ugly ones as the bad guys. But I don't think real life works that way. A guy can be totally hot and still be evil." She chomped into her sandwich as though biting someone's head off.

"Are we still talking about Charlie?"

Amanda shook her head. "Healey," she mumbled, her mouth full.

"What did Healey do?"

The young woman scowled. "Had sex with me."

"Oh, my God, Amanda, he didn't…"

She waved a hand and shook her head. "No. Picked him up at Emo's. But he was only there because he followed me. He was doing his job. He shouldn't have let me pick him up." She looked angry, but Lexy also saw the hurt in her eyes.

"Bastard."

"Yeah."

"Is he here?"

"No. He stayed behind in New York. Charlie had stuff for him to do, but I swear, Lexy, I love you like a sister but I would not have gotten on a plane with that man."

"Don't blame you. Did he have any explanation for why he let you, ah, pick him up?"

"Oh, the usual. It's not what you think, I have feelings for you, give me another chance, the usual bullshit." She waved her hand as though swatting a mosquito.

"I can't—"

"Forget about it. How 'bout you? You and Charlie tried out the Lyons Stagecoach yet?"

"No. And I will never forgive you for making me tell Charlie my favorite sexual position."

She got an unrepentant grin in return. "Has he teased you about it?"

"No. He never said a word."

"Huh. Maybe he doesn't know what it is."

Lexy licked butter from her thumb. "Charlie looks like a guy who knows every move in the Kama Sutra. And a few more."

"Yeah. I think so, too. He hasn't mentioned the Lyons Stagecoach, he hasn't teased you about knowing your favorite sex position." She shook her head. "That's not good."

"Why? What do you think it means?"

"Wild guess? He's planning to ride in your stagecoach." She stood up and moved her body provocatively until they were both snorting with laughter.

"Come on," Lexy said at last. "We've got work to do."

Some time later Amanda said, "So, are you going to let him?"

Lexy raised her gaze from the magnifier. "Ride my coach? I haven't decided yet."

"At least he didn't lie to you."

"No. He only kidnapped me. His excuse is he did it to save my life."

"Men. They always have some story."

"Yeah. Pass me that hammer."

12

"YOU SURE YOU KNOW HOW to fly this thing?" Lexy asked as the twin-engine Cessna chugged its way up into the sky. Maybe if they were in Kansas wheeling over flat fields of corn she wouldn't have her heart backing up into her throat, but in Colorado? The little plane had to fight its way up over the Rockies. Charlie seemed pretty calm, which she guessed was a good thing, except he always seemed calm.

"Enjoy the view," he said.

Which didn't exactly answer her question. She turned and rolled her eyes at Amanda, buckled into one of the backseats and seeming a lot more at home in the small plane than she felt.

"So, what's the plan when we get back to New York?"

"A simple one. We're doing some shopping. We've got a little prep work to do before the gala. And then we're going to hide out where no one will find us."

"Mexico?"

He glanced at her, looking very piloty with his headset. "The Plaza."

"You're insane."

"Probably."

He didn't seem nearly as bothered by her accusation as she was, but then he had all the power in this relationship.

For now.

She was nothing if not a fighter and so long as they seemed to be on the same side, she was content—well, resigned—to the idea of him in her life. Temporarily.

She didn't want to distract the man while he was flying a plane, so she took his advice and stared out the window. The plane hit a patch of turbulence and bounced up and down a couple of times. It had been doing that for most of the trip and she had to force herself not to squawk.

The peaks were snowcapped and jagged, gorgeous in the sunshine as they flew east toward New York.

What Pendegraff had planned seemed bold to the point of insanity, but she had to admit the idea of walking into the lion's den and out again wearing the very jewels Grayson coveted was exciting.

Besides, she had a score to settle with Mr. Grayson.

She raised her voice to be heard above the noise of the engine and the wind rattling at the windows. The idea of waltzing into the Plaza and going to a fancy charity gala all while she was presumed dead seemed absurd and oddly satisfying. "I hope Grayson has a heart attack when he sees us."

"But not fatal. I want him in jail."

She smiled. Maybe they could work together after all.

They landed without incident; in fact Lexy had a reluctant admiration for how easily he brought the small plane down into the private airfield.

After filling out some paperwork in the office they walked out the other side.

Lexy's step hitched when she recognized the limo waiting for them. "Last time I rode in that thing it didn't end so well."

Amanda also stalled when she caught sight of the driver. "Oh, no."

Pendegraff put a hand on each lower back and urged the women on. "Don't be too hard on Healey. He kept a good eye on Amanda. And he's making sure we have some people we can trust on security tomorrow."

The driver moved to the rear door as they approached and opened it, very properly. She slid inside the familiar interior.

She heard him say, "Amanda? Why don't you ride up front, with me?"

"In your dreams." And Amanda got into the back.

Charlie slid in beside Lexy. "Everything all set?" he asked.

"Yes," the man in front said and slid him a hotel key folder.

The March day was gray and overcast, already depressing, and the thought of everyone here at home thinking she was dead didn't do a thing to make her feel better. There was something about returning to New York that made her current dilemma more real to her than it had appeared when she'd seen the news reports. Here she was. She could ask the driver to take her home, but she had no home. All her stuff, from her clothes to her tools to her tax returns. Gone.

She supposed she was in shock of some sort because she felt numb. Everything was gone and she didn't seem able to grasp what that meant for the immediate future.

She leaned forward. "Could we drive past my studio?"

Healey glanced instinctively at Charlie, who shot her a concerned glance. "You know you can't stop or go inside."

"I know. I need to see the place, to make it real. I feel like the fire was something that happened in a TV show, that it's fiction, not that my home and business are really gone."

"Okay." He spoke to Healey. "Don't even slow. Cruise by and—" to her "—don't even think about putting down a window. We're only doing this because no one will see you through the tinted glass."

"Okay." He didn't have to do this, so she managed a small smile. "Thanks."

The limo cruised through the insanity of midtown traffic. After the utter peace of the mountains, the honking and sirens and noise of millions of people living their lives seemed loud and jarring, even in the relative quiet of the limo.

As they got closer to SoHo, her spine began to tingle. It was a stress reaction she'd had since she was a teenager. Her stomach felt strange, too, as though she were coming down with something.

The streets grew familiar, her neighborhood was upon them busy with shoppers and tourists and the residents of the area. Her neighbors and customers.

She all but pressed her face to the glass of the window, straining for the first glimpse of her place. Maybe they'd played some kind of cruel joke on her, maybe her studio was standing, its bright blue door as inviting as ever. Her store full of customers buying her ready-to-wear collection and ordering custom pieces.

Then she saw it.

She didn't realize she'd made a sound until she heard a cry of distress bounce through the air.

A warm hand took hers in a hard grasp and she held on tight to Charlie.

Amanda didn't say a word. In fact, she didn't even turn her head, as though she couldn't bear to look.

Traffic crawled so Lexy had plenty of time to take in the bubbled, blackened paint, the broken windows, the dirty trickles where the fire hoses had done their work. Charred beams were visible, her pretty window display a sooty mess.

Crime scene tape stretched across the doorway and yellow wooden barriers kept the pedestrians streaming around the building—she supposed there was some danger that something could fall on them from above. But her home and business were like an infected patient no one would go near.

From nowhere, tears blurred her vision and clogged her throat. That was her life, her business, her future. Black, burned, over.

There were commissions, of course. Clients and customers who had hired her to do a job. Her spine straightened against the leather upholstery as hot, cleansing anger roared through her, sweeping away her feelings of loss and self-pity.

She would do her job. She'd finish those commissions, just as soon as she and Pendegraff nailed whoever was responsible for this senseless destruction.

"You okay?" he said softly beside her.

She shook her head. Not ready yet for anyone to see her face. "But I'm angry. And getting angrier by the minute. I want whoever did this nailed. And I'll do whatever it takes to make sure that happens."

"That's the spirit."

He squeezed her hand and let go and she missed the warmth, the sense that he might be a thief and a kidnapper and a thousand other things she wouldn't approve of, but for some reason, she trusted him.

"Let's get to the hotel and get planning."

"Can I go home?" Amanda asked. "I need to check my messages and water my plants."

Charlie asked Healey, "Can she?"

The man in the front nodded. "Nobody's shown any interest. She should be fine. I'll keep an eye on her."

Amanda narrowed her gaze. "You stay away from me or I'll call the cops."

Suddenly the limo jerked sideways, pulled over to a curb and Healey turned around. Lexy had never seen him show expression before, so his anger was impressive. "Charlie, how long have I been working for you?"

"About five years."

"And in those five years have I ever had sex with one of our clients, or anybody remotely connected to our business?"

"No."

Amanda made a rude noise. "And I would believe that why?"

"Because it's true," Charlie said. "Amanda, I'm as pissed off with Healey as you are. What he did was dangerous, unprofessional and completely out of character for him. I can only assume that he's lost his mind or he has feelings for you." He turned to the driver. "Which is it, Healey?"

The man glared at all three of them in the back. "There's nothing wrong with my mind," he informed them with dignity. Then faced forward and pulled the limo back out into traffic.

13

THE PLAZA WAS LIKE Central Park, or the MoMA, or Saks, part of the fabric of her life, but not a place where Lexy spent a lot of time. She'd had brunch or drinks at the Plaza a few times, but she'd never even seen one of the guest rooms, so even with the sick feeling in the pit of her stomach since she'd seen the fire damage, she still managed a jolt of anticipation as they entered the landmark hotel.

Charlie didn't check in. It seemed Healey had done so on his behalf. He didn't even explain the room arrangements to her, but he wasn't a man who wasted a lot of words. She supposed she'd soon find out what was going on.

The elevator made its expensively quiet ascent to the eighteenth floor. Charlie strode to the door of their room as though he was a regular visitor. Maybe he was.

When he opened the door he stepped aside for her to enter first. She thought those kind of manners were so inbred he didn't even think about his actions.

It was nice.

She entered and her jaw dropped. "Are you kidding me? This is a suite."

"Yes."

She stepped in and glanced around. "I feel like I'm in Versailles."

The old-world charm of the room was distinctly European in flavor. No simple bedroom this; it was a full two-bedroom suite including butler's pantry, and two sumptuous bathrooms, so any idea she'd had that Pendegraff had more than business in mind could be put away for now.

They stood there for a moment. She'd unpack, but she didn't have any luggage.

"What do we do now?" she asked.

"We shop."

"That sounds great since I have no clothes whatsoever and certainly Cinderella has nothing to wear to the ball tomorrow night, but I thought you wanted me to stay hidden?"

"I do. The shopping is coming to us."

"Rich people really do have different rules of life."

He put the black briefcase he was carrying on the table and carried a black leather bag into one of the bedrooms. "You seem pretty hung up about rich people. We're not all that different, you know."

"Putting aside our different views on morality, you fly your own plane, you book a suite at the Plaza on a whim, you don't go shopping, you bring people to you, I'd say we have nothing in common." She sighed, flopping back into the luxury that was the couch. "My mom and dad always worked hard. They took pride in that, and so do I. I guess I don't have a lot of respect for people who lounge around all day living on trust funds." She flicked him a glance. "Not to be rude."

"Of course not."

There was a discreet knock on the door. He glanced at his watch. "Right on schedule."

When he opened the door and a stylish middle-aged woman sailed in with two assistants, a rolling wardrobe rack, boxes and several wardrobe bags, Lexy felt a spurt of annoyance. Where did he get off snapping his fingers and getting all this special treatment? Money, that's how, and not honestly earned money, either.

The woman had a slight French accent and introduced herself as Francine. Her helpers she ignored. She didn't seem to need any introduction to Charlie and was so uninterested in any details about Lexy that she almost choked not being able to tell the woman who she was and why she was here. She had no choice but to let these people think she was another Pendegraff possession, a mistress to be decorated and dressed according to his lordship's whims.

Her temper simmered while Francine fawned all over Charlie, who seemed accustomed to the attention and not at all bothered by it. She motioned one of the helpers to the closet and after some zipping sounds and a few soft directions, she returned with her assistant holding two dresses, one in each hand.

"Black or color?" Both dresses were beautiful. She suspected Charlie had insisted on a simple gown with a low neck to showcase the emeralds. From the fact that Francine was willing to run all over town with a selection of dresses for a private showing, Lexy had to assume they were devastatingly expensive.

Charlie considered them both, then turned his gaze to her. She ought to be amused, but the way he sized her up as though he'd seen her naked a hundred times and owned her body incensed her.

"Black, I think," he said.

"I prefer color," she snapped. She was determined to have some say in choosing her own dress.

His slightly amused expression told her he'd read her mind. "Try them all on," he instructed.

She stomped into the bedroom that didn't contain his bag, only hanging on to the shreds of her temper in the knowledge that she needed to be dressed properly for the gala in order to catch Grayson tomorrow.

One of the assistants followed her in and opened a display case full of lingerie.

Lexy's annoyance melted like ice cream on a hot sidewalk. "Oh, my," she said, leaning forward to touch the exquisite filmy things in the case.

"Monsieur said you were thirty-four B but I brought a few sizes."

"Monsieur was right," and the fact that he'd checked her out so thoroughly was mildly unnerving.

The helper's name was Marie-Anne and she became Lexy's new *bff* as they matched lingerie with the first dress, a long black evening gown paired with black high heels.

The moment she was in the first of the dresses, she knew the style was wrong. It was a one-shoulder arrangement that drew attention to the sweep of fabric from shoulder to hip. Jewelry would be overkill in this dress. She was about to shake her head and step out of it when she thought, what the heck? Mr. Pendegraff wanted to sit around and look at dresses? She'd oblige. She'd never known a man who hadn't grown bored in five minutes of shopping with a woman. Let's see how Charlie liked a parade of dresses, spaced out as he waited for her to change. And she didn't plan to hurry.

She walked slowly out into the main room.

Francine immediately launched into an effusive gush of praise about how beautiful it was, what a magnificent figure mademoiselle had, but she ignored the woman and concentrated on Charlie's reaction.

Lexy was female and vain enough to be gratified at the way his eyes grew intent as they looked at her, at the drape of fabric that accentuated her curves, but his verdict was the same as hers.

"I've got a fine necklace I want you to wear, darling. You definitely need something with a lower neckline."

"All right, sweetheart," she murmured in the way she imagined a well-pampered mistress might. Not that she had any experience in the matter, or desire to find out.

She found the perfect dress on the third try. The gown could have been designed for her, so lovingly did it hug her curves, accentuating her small breasts, and leaving her shoulders bare. It was an antique-gold color, which would highlight the necklace to perfection. She looked delicate and slightly mysterious. She'd never worn a prettier dress. Or, she suspected, a more expensive one.

"It's perfect," Marie-Anne whispered. "Like it was made for you."

"I know." And she slipped the dress off.

"You're not going to show monsieur?"

"Yes, I'm going to show monsieur. But we should save the best for last, don't you think?"

The Frenchwoman shrugged in a "who can understand Americans" kind of way, and pulled out the next dress.

"I always think it's good to keep a man waiting, don't you?"

A very Gallic shrug of the shoulders. "Some men,

yes. But this one? I would not care to cross him, mademoiselle."

"How funny. I'm absolutely looking forward to it."

14

How could women stand shopping? Charles wondered as he tried his hardest not to look bored and to continue to speak politely to Francine. He had a strong suspicion that Lexy was dragging this thing out as long as she could to make him suffer. And it was working.

After the fifth dress he was ready to cry truce. Enough already. She looked fabulous in all of them, as she must know, but still she insisted that this one wasn't quite perfect. The hem was too frilly, the fabric not what she had in mind, the neckline too high, too low, too wide, too wavy, frumpy, décolletage and he'd lost track of what else was wrong. He felt like yelling to her that all the dress had to do was show off the emeralds, she was meant to be a frame, that was all. But she already knew that, which was why he was pretty sure she was yanking his chain.

He guessed he deserved retribution. He'd kidnapped her, as she kept on reminding him, which seemed to trump the fact that he'd also saved her life.

Women.

"I think this is the last one," Francine said in her smooth way as though she could read his boredom.

"Good."

The door opened behind him. He turned his head.

And felt his eyes bug out. Totally cartoon style. Wowza.

He'd imagined he'd seen everything a dress could do to that sweet little body, but he had been wrong.

The dress didn't just fit her, it caressed her when she moved, making a man want to put his hands in all the places the fabric was allowed to linger and he wasn't.

Off the shoulder, low-cut, her bosom was a white expanse waiting for the perfect jewelry.

Once you got past the small, shapely breasts, the dress showed him a trim waist without an ounce of fat, and curvy hips. He wanted to say something but he felt as if his tongue was welded to the roof of his mouth.

Even Francine's gushing actually sounded genuine this time. She oohed, and ahhed and ooh-la-la-d and still he stared, dumbfounded.

Being in such close quarters with a beautiful woman and not being allowed to touch her had been an effort from the moment he saw her, but now that he'd seen her in this dress, he didn't think he'd be able to stop himself wanting her. Who was he kidding, anyway? Since he'd been fool enough to kiss her, he couldn't get the feel of her body out of his mind, the taste of her, the way her lips fit against his.

Lexy ignored the fussing Frenchwoman and concentrated on him. Finally, when he still hadn't spoken, she said, "You like?"

He nodded. Enthusiastically.

Her amusement deepened. "You speechless?"

He nodded again.

"Good," she said, her lips smiling in a mysterious fashion that hid her thoughts. "I like that in my dates."

She nodded brusquely and he was reminded that she was a very competent businesswoman. "We'll take this one. Including the shoes and lingerie I'm wearing."

"An excellent choice, mademoiselle."

"I'm also going to need two pairs of jeans, some shirts and some everyday underwear. Marie-Anne knows me pretty well by now. She can pick them out for me. Could you have them delivered today?"

"With pleasure, mademoiselle."

When the women had all but bowed themselves out, Lexy said, "I could get used to being a kept woman." She contemplated her new shoes. Then struck a sultry pose in front of the long mirror. The vision made him instantly, humiliatingly hard.

"I've never been a mistress before."

"Not to burst your bubble, but there's more to being a mistress than shopping." He eyed her hungrily. "There are certain…services you're expected to provide."

Her gaze rose and connected with his and passion flared as it did pretty much every time they were close.

"Catch me a killer and we'll see what we can do about that."

"That's a pretty tall order."

"Oh, believe me, I'm worth it."

He had no trouble believing it.

LEXY WENT BACK TO HER bedroom and slipped off the most gorgeous dress she'd ever worn. Not that she didn't have a certain style all her own, but she tended to vintage pieces and young designers she knew who were just starting out. She'd even been known to barter jewels for frocks. But this? This dress was in a whole other league. Charlie's league.

She shook her head, hanging it carefully in the closet and pulling her jeans and one of the shirts from Colorado back on.

She swept back into the living room to find Charlie immersed in his computer.

He glanced up when she entered the room and politely stopped what he was doing.

"Maybe you could Google the guest list. I'll need a rundown of all the inbred, pampered socialites I'll be rubbing shoulders with. Bare shoulders, too. I hope my plebian roots don't freak them out."

"You know what your problem is? You're a snob."

She drew in her breath so fast she almost choked on it. "I am not. I'm working class and proud of it."

"Exactly. That's what I meant. You look down your nose at me because I have a certain background and possessions without knowing anything about who I truly am."

"That is blatantly untrue. I know you're a thief."

He crossed his arms over his chest and sat back. "What else do you know about me?"

"Aside from the fact that you're arrogant, pushy and annoying, what more do I need to know?"

"Right back at you, sweetheart."

She went to the kitchen to make tea. After a minute, she said, "I'm nervous. It makes me bitchy. Sorry."

She didn't realize he'd moved until she heard him behind her say, "Don't be nervous. It's going to be fine."

"I'm going to walk under Edward Grayson's nose wearing the necklace his mistress stole from him, the one he murdered her for stealing."

"Allegedly."

"Well, I am allegedly nervous."

"You don't have to do it."

"I said I'm nervous, not that I'm a quitter. Of course we're doing it. I like the audacity of the plan."

He gripped her shoulders. "That's the spirit. Look, I need to go out for a few hours. Will you be okay?"

"Why? Where are you going?"

"Some business to attend to."

"Aren't you afraid I'll run away?"

He turned to her, his eyebrows lifting in surprise. "Are you planning to run away?"

"Probably not." He didn't point out the obvious. That she didn't have a lot of places to go.

"But I'm going to call my father."

He nodded. "Great idea. Tell him to come by. I'd like to meet him."

"You would?"

"Sure."

"But he's a cop."

"So you said."

"And you're a thief." She made an up-and-down motion with her two hands. "Cop, thief, I'm seeing a conflict of interest here."

"Oh, we're on the same side on some things."

"Such as catching Grayson?"

The look he sent her was inscrutable. "Among other things." He came forward and kissed her swiftly. "Use the peephole before you open the door."

After he left, she was restless. Keyed up. Her spine continued to tingle. What happened over the next twenty-four hours would be critical. And she had to trust a man who was a thief and a kidnapper. Not exactly a résumé that filled her with confidence. And yet, oddly, she'd come to trust this man.

Half an hour later, her clothes arrived. If it wasn't the full Julia Roberts wardrobe from *Pretty Woman,* the clothing she'd asked for was a lot more practical. She wasn't planning to attend any polo matches or fancy dinners while she was here, only the one gala, then she'd have to go back to rebuilding her business. And her life.

Marie-Anne brought her the jeans she'd asked for, a couple of shirts, sweaters, a tweed car coat, walking shoes and a pair of boots. There was even a funky scarf to wear with the coat. "This is great, thanks."

"You're welcome." The woman hesitated. "I know you said your luggage went missing."

"Yeah. Stupid airline. Still haven't found it."

"I was wondering if you also need some makeup."

She slapped a hand over her mouth. "Yes. I totally forgot."

A quick smile. "We sell these kits at the store. It's not everything you need, but it's a start."

"Thank you so much." She gave the woman an impulsive hug.

The next visitor was her father, who enveloped her in a crushing hug the second the door shut behind him. She knew he was emotional from the way he squeezed her so tight she thought her ribs would snap.

"Don't ever put me through anything like that again," he warned.

"No. It was awful."

He set her away from him and glanced around. He wasn't a tall man but he was solid and she could feel his temper simmering. "Where is he? Where's the guy who put my baby in danger?"

He stalked around the suite long enough to figure out that there were two bedrooms and her things were in one while Charlie's were in the other. It helped cool his temper a degree or two.

"He had to go out for a while but he said he's looking forward to meeting you."

Her dad grunted, never a good sign. "I got a few things I want to say to him."

"Do you want some tea or coffee or something?"

He shook his head.

She sat beside him on the couch. "Tell me everything you've found out."

"You were right. That name you gave me? Tiffany Starr? How'd you know she was the dead girl?"

"It's a complicated story."

"I got all afternoon."

So she told him how the woman and her supposed mother had come into her studio, the story they'd given her and she told him about the emeralds.

"Seems to me there's some details you're leaving out."

"The rest of the story is Charlie's. He'll have to tell you himself. He should be back any minute."

Her father looked very grim. She hadn't seen him like this since her mom died. She put a hand on his arm. "What is it, Dad?"

"That girl was murdered."

Even though she'd suspected this news, it was like a blow to the gut. "Oh, no." She swallowed, had to know. "How?"

"She was shot."

"Oh, poor woman."

"It gets worse."

"Worse? What could be worse than being murdered and then burned?"

"She was killed with your gun."

15

LEXY'S HORRIFIED GAZE flew to her father's. "What?"

He had his cop face on, but she knew him so well. He was angry, frustrated, confused. And a little bit helpless, which he would hate more than anything.

"She was killed with my gun? That means, oh, God, that means she was still alive when they brought her to my place. They killed her there." Then the implications of the murder weapon struck her. "Dad, am I a suspect?"

"Of course you're not a suspect," he barked at her.

She licked her lips, thinking back to that terrible night. "But I had my gun out that night. There'd be fresh prints." She remembered threatening Charlie with the gun, the pounding and breaking glass in her front studio that had distracted her long enough for him to overpower her and grab the weapon. But Charlie, consummate thief that he was, had been wearing gloves. And she'd be willing to bet that whoever else had handled her gun, whoever had killed Tiffany Starr, had also worn gloves.

She felt like she was twelve again and in trouble. Only this time she knew her trouble was serious. She found herself pleading her innocence. "I'd never met the woman until that day. She came in and gave me a false name. She wanted an expensive necklace reset. A necklace she stole. But why would they use my gun?"

"You got any idea who might have killed her?"

They were interrupted by the door opening. Charlie came in, took one look at her face and strode to her side. "What is it?" He held out his hands and without even thinking, she put hers into them. His clasp felt warm and reassuring.

"They used my gun to kill that poor woman."

"Bastards."

"You mind telling me who you are and what you know about all this?" her father commanded.

"Oh, Dad, I'm sorry," she said before Charlie could speak. She released his hands. "Charles Pendegraff, meet my father, Jed Dabrowski."

Charlie extended a hand. "Pleased to meet you, sir."

Ignoring the hand, her father stood and glared at Charlie. "If anything happens to my Lexy while she's with you, I'll shoot you dead."

"Dad—"

Letting his hand drop back to his side, Charlie pulled himself up to his full height. "If anything happens to Lexy while she's with me, I'll load the gun myself."

The two men stared at each other, both tense and wary, and then to her amazement her father nodded, once, like he'd made up his mind about something. His prizefighter stance relaxed. "Good. We understand each other."

He sat down on the luxurious couch and motioned them to do the same. "Now, suppose you tell me what the hell is going on?"

And, to her amazement, Charlie did. He explained that he'd been hired to retrieve the stones, and pretty much gave a full description of everything he knew and everything that had happened up to and including the moment she caught him stealing the necklace.

At this point, she took over the story before Charlie did anything stupid like incriminate himself. "Charlie saved my life, Dad. He got me out of there and convinced me to get right out of New York with him." She didn't tell her father that he'd "convinced" her using unorthodox methods.

"Damn it, Lex, you shoulda come to me," her father said.

"I'm sorry, Dad. I wasn't thinking straight." Ha, and wasn't that the truth. At the time, she hadn't been thinking at all. She'd been drugged into unconsciousness.

"It would have been a good thing if you had. Well, you're not a suspect, but they'd sure like you to come down to the station and give a statement."

"And I will. But not until after the gala. They wrecked my place and now it turns out they killed that woman in my home. Using my gun. I am so bringing that Grayson down."

"I'll help you," Charlie said.

There was a tense pause. She looked at her father with appeal in her eyes.

"And so will I," her father echoed.

And suddenly they were a team.

Another knock sounded on the door. She stiffened.

"That'll be Healey," Charlie said.

He rose and opened the door to Healey, who came in and swept a swift glance around the room, as though checking for weapons, before entering. Amanda came in behind him. She held herself stiffly away from him. *Wow,* Lexy thought, *she really doesn't like this guy.*

"Healey, this is Jed Dabrowski, Lexy's father. Jed, Healey's my associate. And I assume you know Amanda?"

The two men shook hands, sizing each other up as they did so. The suite seemed to be pulsing with testosterone all of a sudden.

Thank heaven for Amanda, Lexy thought as her father said, "Hi, sweetheart," and enveloped her in one of his bear hugs.

They sat around the ornate living area sharing information, and throwing out ideas.

"I want my daughter protected," her dad said.

"Absolutely." Charlie turned to Healey. "How many security guards do they usually hire for the Diamond Ball?"

"They call in twenty men from a private security firm. Six outside making sure nobody gets in who shouldn't be there and that the guests get inside the mansion with all their jewels intact and back to their limos. Another six patrol the grounds and eight men work the interior. In addition, Grayson has a few permanent employees who wander around."

"Okay. Could be better, could be worse. But I think we can make it work."

He glanced at Jed. "I'm guessing, based on the bling at these events, that the NYPD has some kind of presence?"

"Sure. But I don't get involved in that kinda crap."

"This year, I think you should. See if you can get assigned to the detail. Lexy and I will both feel better if you're on the premises."

"Consider it done. Anybody who doesn't already owe me a favor, soon will."

"Excellent."

Jed Dabrowski was looking at Charlie through narrowed eyes. "You've got something in mind?"

"Yeah. How 'bout I bring in some pizzas and we'll go over the plan?"

So they sat over pizza and sodas making plans, contingency plans, thinking of everything that could go wrong and how to prevent disaster.

Hearing Charlie explain the details to someone new, she realized how simple his plan was. So simple she almost laughed. Except that nothing about murder and arson was funny.

After everyone left, there was a moment of awkwardness. She didn't know what to do. It was nine-thirty, too early to go to bed, too strange to sit out here chatting with Charlie.

He seemed equally restless. He picked up a sports magazine, put it down.

Finally she said, "I apologize for my father. He's very old school. You hurt his daughter and there'll be hell to pay."

"I respect his position. He seems like a good man."

Her lips relaxed into a smile. "He is a good man. But tact was never his strong suit."

"He's worried about you."

"I know."

"Damn it, he's right. Lexy, you don't have to do this. I was crazy to suggest it. I'll find another way."

"Hey, I'm in this, too. Grayson burned down my house and business, remember?"

"Grayson's a dangerous man."

"So it seems. But he'll be in a public venue with no

idea that I'll show up with his necklace on. What can he possibly do to us?"

"I don't know, but I don't want anything to happen to you."

"Hey, you're not getting sentimental on me, are you?"

"No. Don't want your father using me for target practice."

He came closer, looked as though he were going to reach for her and then suddenly turned away. "Think I'll get an early night. Busy day tomorrow."

And he was gone.

16

SHE WAS KEYED UP, excited, nervous and—if she was honest with herself—a little nauseated.

She was like a little kid, getting ready hours too early for a birthday party. Charlie was mysteriously gone again and so she'd indulged in a bubble bath, shaved and plucked and polished herself. The manicurist, hairdresser and makeup artist had already been and she'd slipped on the lacy black underwear. All she was waiting for was the time to crawl along so she could slip into her dress.

Her freshly manicured fingers drummed against the upholstery. She tried to read the paper, but she couldn't concentrate. She flipped on the television, flicked a few channels and then punched the off button.

She considered having a drink to calm her nerves, but decided she'd better keep a clear head for tonight.

She opened the closet and considered the dress hanging there. It wasn't simply a dress. It was a net to catch a killer. The Isabella Emeralds the bait.

And they planned to snag a very sharp-toothed shark tonight.

She put a hand to her stomach. Phew. Pressed her lips together and the unfamiliar thickness of lipstick on her mouth reminded her of the unfamiliar amount of cosmetics she was wearing. The makeup felt oddly protective like a mask.

The shoes were in their box sitting on the bottom of the closet. She eased the box open, slipped the shoes on. Maybe if she walked around the suite in the unfamiliar gold heels it would ensure she was smoother tonight. At least the activity would give her something useful to do while she waited for time to pass, for Charlie to return, for the big night to begin.

She walked around the suite once, twice, until it felt more like pacing than walking.

Then she heard the key in the door.

Thank goodness.

It opened and Charlie walked in. He caught sight of her and it seemed as though he stopped, going completely still. He glanced at her hair, her face and all the way down to her new shoes. "I see the salon people have been," he said at last in that lazy drawl.

The air between them felt suddenly electric and she'd never been more conscious that she was wearing nothing but a hotel robe and, under it, the skimpiest lingerie imported from France and a pair of gold heels.

"I always get ready early. It's a curse. Then I have nothing to do with myself."

"You look beautiful," he said. It didn't sound entirely like a compliment, more like an inconvenience.

"Thanks."

He went to the hotel safe, punched in the code and popped the door. Out came the jewelry case that had started this nightmare. He opened the case and brought it to her.

The Isabella Emeralds.

"The jewels will look spectacular against your skin," he said, like a connoisseur considering a painting for his house.

"I usually wear my own creations when I go out socially. It's good advertising."

He smiled briefly, stepping closer to her. "Next time I take you out, I promise you can wear your own merchandise. For tonight, you'll have to settle for the emeralds."

Even though she'd seen them, studied them, copied them, she was still awestruck by the brilliance and clarity of the gems. By the setting that was so perfect. The intricate setting that was both ornate and delicate had been designed and executed by a master craftsman. She'd handled a few pieces that might compare in value but never anything that also had historical importance, or that she would actually wear.

"Do you know the legend?" he said as he carefully lifted the glittering mass from its case.

She'd read everything she could find on the set and was fairly certain she knew the legend to which he was referring, but she chose to say, "Which legend?"

Charlie moved behind her, nudged her until she could see herself in the ornate mirror. Her hair was styled in a simple knot to keep it out of the way. She wanted nothing to distract the eye from the necklace.

As he moved behind her she felt his presence, felt the heat coming off his body, his breath stirring the skin at her nape. She felt the coolness of the stones and metal as they rested against her upper chest, under the white hotel robe.

"There's a story that Isabella wanted so badly to finance Columbus's voyage to the new world that she pawned her jewelry to raise the cash."

He fingered the gems at her throat. "Among the other bounty he brought her, this gift was a nice repayment for her pawned stones."

They both watched the green wink in the mirror. "I've rarely seen such a deep green but it's characteristic of emeralds originating from the ancient Muzo mines of Colombia."

The thought that Christopher Columbus had handled these gems, that Queen Isabella of Spain had worn them around her own neck, sent a thrill through Lexy.

"It's also rumored that the stones inflamed the royal lust, giving her back the pleasure of youth."

As he spoke, his fingers traced her collarbone, softly caressed the skin of her shoulders and neck in a gesture that felt both intimate and arousing.

"You made that up," she said, her voice not much more than a whisper.

"Want me to cite my sources?"

She felt her breath hitch. He was so close. His fingers were smooth and sure as they fastened the complicated clasp.

"Magnificent," he said, his words stirring her hair. Their gazes connected in the mirror and it was as though an electric storm passed through her.

She felt transfixed, mute, could neither turn around nor throw out some flip remark. Instead she remained rooted to the spot, feeling her breath grow shallow. With every breath she felt the weight of the gems, could see the flash of light, the deep green and hot white diamond spark in the reflection. She needed the extra makeup, she realized, to match the drama of the jewels, and the sophisticated side twist of hair was perfect.

In slow motion she watched as Charlie eased the fluffy white robe to the side, revealing the jewels in their full glory. He didn't remove his hands, so she felt the heat of his fingers burn into her flesh.

He bent closer, his eyes growing heavy with an emotion she recognized as desire because it so neatly mirrored her own. In slow motion she saw his lips come nearer, felt his breath on her shoulder and then the soft, warm press of his lips. "I've tried to stay away from you, but I don't think I can do it any longer."

A tiny tremulous sigh escaped her lips and she felt his curve slightly as he pressed his mouth to the pulse beating at her throat.

"You arouse me, bewitch me, make me crazy with wanting you."

"Oh, yes," she whispered in a voice she barely recognized. Must be all the stress, she thought dimly, causing both of them to act so crazy. She felt the light stubble of his beard as he kissed his slow way up to her ear, then whispered, "You are so beautiful. I want you."

His clever thief's hands then moved, tracing the front of her robe to the sash, which he slowly untied, pulling the edges apart and revealing her in the deliciously lacy bra and panties.

The robe fell to the floor and it was his turn to make an incomprehensible sound, half sigh, half moan.

Her body was on fire; she felt as much on display as the gems and the experience was intoxicating. "I want you, too."

He touched her slowly, carefully, like a man who appreciates art and takes what he wants without asking permission. She saw herself being touched, watched his hands tracing the shape of her breasts through the filmy lingerie. His fingers looked dark against her pale skin.

He was fully dressed standing behind her, dark and serious but for the gleaming eyes that showed how close to the edge of passion he was.

"This is a terrible idea," she said.

"I know." And then he turned her around and pulled her into his arms, kissing her so hard she felt the breath squeeze out of her. His arms held her tight, hands running up and down her back as though he couldn't get enough of her.

Her passion flared brighter than the flash of the gems as she ground herself against him, panting against his mouth, opening to him, offering generously and taking greedily at the same time.

She wanted everything, all of him, and she needed it now. His erection was strong and hard as she reached between them for his belt buckle.

He toed off his shoes, she tugged at his shirt. A jagged scar on his shoulder caught her attention as she pulled the shirt off him; she pressed her lips to the spot, tasting heat and salt on his skin.

He dragged his boxers off, and then he was naked and magnificent before her.

He sucked her through the lacy bra, making her moan as her tingling nipples sprang to life. He peeled the lacy thong down her legs, then rose slowly, kissing whatever part of her was in reach of his mouth, her knee, her upper thigh, her belly, her breasts and finally her mouth, kissing her deeply while he reached between them and began to play in her curls, finding her slick and hot. When he rubbed her clit she found herself thrusting forward into his hand; when he pushed a finger inside her she cried out.

In her lust-fogged brain she managed to pant, "condom," and he sped to the bathroom, returning with a package, which he ripped open as he ran back. In seconds he was sheathed and then his hot length was pressing against her, her arms wrapped around his neck. He scooped her up, and she opened for him, wrapping her legs around his waist. He backed her up to the wall, and with his eyes open on hers, thrust up and inside her body.

Oh, he felt so good, so absolutely right as he pushed deeply inside her, giving her a moment to adjust before moving, driving her up, up, until she was wild for release, her hips riding against him, her breasts pressed hard against his chest, the necklace pressing against their hearts.

Their mouths were fused, their bodies locked together and as they moved with a kind of frantic desperation she felt the delicious ache begin to spread, build, until she shattered against him, crying out into his mouth, feeling her body busting with light.

He muttered nonsense words against her mouth and then she felt him stiffen and cry out as he climaxed deep inside her.

She felt boneless as she slid down the wall and back to her feet, though she still needed to hold on to him as she was afraid she'd collapse to the floor if she didn't.

He didn't let her go. He was breathing heavily, his heart thumping hard against hers. She stroked his back, waited for both of them to come back down to earth.

She tilted her head back, eyed him through half-closed eyes. "Maybe I believe in that legend after all," she said.

17

AMANDA'S CELL PHONE RANG. Healey again. She was about to turn the thing off and then decided to answer it. Maybe if she told him once and for all to leave her alone, he would.

"What do you want?" she snapped.

"What was I supposed to do?" he snapped right back. "You came onto me, remember? Sure, I could have blown you off, and then you know what you would have done?"

"Gone home. Alone." She squeezed her eyes shut, knowing it was a lie.

"Bullshit. You'd have found some other willing stud. And you know what? I couldn't stand the thought. I'd been watching you, okay? Not because I'm a pervert but because it was my job. You were lost and grieving and messed up."

She opened her mouth to blast him. But he was right. So right. "I know," she said softly.

"And I was seriously attracted to you."

"You were?"

"Yeah." A pause. "Still am."

"Oh. Are you still my bodyguard?"

"No, ma'am. I'm off the case."

"Well, thanks for, you know, keeping me safe."

"You're welcome. Now it's just you and me. No job getting in the way. I want to see you again. Start over."

She stifled a smile. "When?"

"How about now? I'm outside your door."

She ran to the peephole. And there he was. Standing outside her door. She figured she had two choices. She could trust him. Or not.

He was so different than anyone she'd ever been with. More serious, way cleaner living, and he really seemed to care about her. Which was probably good.

Also, she hadn't been able to stop thinking about him.

So, she flung open the door and before either of them could speak, they were in each other's arms.

He kicked the door shut behind him. "I missed you," he said into her mouth.

"Me, too." She dragged at his shirt, he stripped off her hoodie, her T-shirt.

Their jeans ended in a single mass on the floor and then they were naked on her unmade bed. Light streamed in the window onto their naked bodies.

She wanted him so badly she literally ached. But he seemed to have other ideas.

He was stroking her in slow, delicious ways, keeping her in the zone but not letting her climax. She groaned, partly from pleasure, partly from sexual frustration and partly from annoyance.

"Are you punishing me?"

He laughed softly. "No. Can't you simply trust me?"

"I have trust issues," she admitted. "From a long string of bad decisions in the guy department."

"How about giving trust another try?"

She hooked a leg over his hip, angled her hips so she could add her own friction. "Will you let me come if I do?"

He grinned down at her. "Maybe."

Her lips curved in response. "I won't make it easy." And then she took over, torturing him until sweat was beading his forehead and he was breathing like a man in pain.

"You gonna let me come?" he finally asked when she'd brought him to the edge and backed off one too many times.

"Maybe."

She put her hand back on him and suddenly found herself flying through the air, hitting the mattress with her back. She squeaked with shock, and found her legs being pushed apart. She gazed up at him, torn between need and satisfaction that she'd won this round. "You in a hurry or something?"

"Yeah." And then he plunged into her. He managed to hold on to his control long enough for her to catch up and she could see the effort it was costing him. He stroked her with his body, stoked her excitement with his own until they hit one of those magic moments where they shattered simultaneously. Usually she closed her eyes at the fateful moment, but she hadn't known how close to climax she was and so was swept away, her gaze locked with his. She felt as if she was looking into the deepest part of him, where all his secrets, his memories and his essence lived.

His eyes went dark, seemed to focus on whatever he

saw inside her open eyes, which she suspected was her secrets, her memories and her essence.

As her orgasm swamped her, she felt a connection so powerful with this man who was a virtual stranger that a mist of tears clouded her vision.

He didn't say anything for a moment, simply held that intimate gaze and then, bending slowly, kissed her. She tasted the salt of his sweat, the softness of his lips and then they were holding each other tight. As though they'd never let go.

When they'd come back to earth, he said, "I'd love to stay and make love to you for days, but I've got to get ready for the gala tonight."

"I know."

"I'm going to go shower." She watched him walk naked to the bathroom, feeling lust stir once more. She was seriously turning into a nymphomaniac.

He paused in the doorway of the bathroom. Didn't turn around. "You staring at my butt?"

Damn, he was good. She could lie, but then he might start wearing clothes around the place. Trust, she reminded herself. Maybe she could trust him with the truth. "Yeah. I am. It's one of your best features."

He chuckled. "Maybe I should turn around and you might want to revise your opinion."

"Egotist. Go shower."

"Come with me."

"Okay."

They made love in the shower, wet and slow. And as they were drying off in her too-small bathroom, bumping into each other, he said, "When this is over, how would you like to go sailing?"

"In March? It would be freezing."

"Not in the Caribbean. I figure both our bosses owe us some time off."

She fought the excitement that roared through her like a flash flood. "You barely know me."

His hand traveled down her spine, tracking the bumps as he went. That hand was warm and sure. "I know the sounds you make when you climax." He dropped a kiss on her damp shoulder.

"I know that when I lick the back of your knees you giggle, and when I touch your sailboat tattoo with my tongue you get goose bumps."

"Do not."

He licked at the tattoo on her back. "Do, too. I know that you're a good person who eats way too much crap and that it makes me happy to wake up with you."

She turned to stare at him. "I've gone out with guys for months, years, who never made a speech half that romantic."

"Bet they were thinking it."

She snorted. "Ah, no."

He kissed her lips softly. "Then they didn't deserve your time. You deserve romance."

"I don't need—" He cut her off with his mouth.

"I know you don't need it, or me, or anyone. You're tough. I get it. So, you don't need romance. I still say you deserve it."

He kissed her one more time and she was embarrassed at the way her hand clung to his shoulder when he pulled away.

He dressed swiftly and she knew that he was going to make sure Charlie and Lexy got in and got away from the gala safely. She wanted to ride along, but she knew it would only look suspicious. She understood she had to stay out of the way even as it killed her to sit home and worry. About all of them.

"I have to go," he said.

"Be careful. And come back tonight."

He kissed her hard. "I'll see you later."

18

Lexy had been to the odd charity gala, of course. Impossible to live in Manhattan and work in the fashion world without ending up at one glitzy benefit or another. But she'd never seen anything like the Diamond Ball hosted by the Graysons. The ball had been going for half a century, but Florence Grayson took over the chairmanship in the late eighties and had held it ever since.

The Diamond Ball raised an enormous sum for charity, but it was also a chance for the rich and connected to polish up the best of their gems and adorn themselves with all the sparkle they owned.

Traditionally they wore diamonds.

She'd wanted to get in these doors for years so she could showcase her own designs to the wealthy, fashionable and fabulous. However, the price tag put the party way beyond her reach. The price of a single ticket was the equivalent of a small car, and a table cost as much as a house in most parts of the country.

If she wasn't slightly apprehensive about being in the company of a possible killer and wearing jewels that were controversial to say the least, she'd have been wildly excited to be here.

Charlie walked at her side, the perfect escort in a Dior tux. They chatted idly as they entered the magnificent ballroom of the Grayson mansion.

"I've always wanted to come to this event," she admitted, trying to ignore the tingle in her spine, "but I've never been able to afford it. I can never pay you back for the cost of my ticket."

He smiled. "Relax. We're both here as guests. We're part of a table."

"A table? I thought those were reserved by big companies and superrich families."

He put a hand to her lower back and urged her forward. "We're here as guests of my mother."

She stopped as though she'd run face-first into a plate-glass window. Smuck.

"What did you just say?"

He seemed amused at her obvious horror. "My mother gets a table every year. She was delighted that I actually accepted her invitation for once. Even more so that I'm bringing a guest."

"I can't meet your mother." Panic was beating at her breast much worse than when she'd thought all she had to deal with was a possible killer. "She'll know what we were doing before we came here tonight. Mothers always know." She put a hand to her hair. "I'm mussed. I'm definitely mussed."

He took her hand in his and lightly kissed it. "You look absolutely perfect," he said, studying her carefully. "I like your hair slightly mussed, and your heavy eyes and swollen lips, you look like you've spent the afternoon being pleasured in my bed, which is exactly how I want you to look. Like a well-pampered mistress."

"Listen, Pendegraff, I don't do mistress. We are equal partners in this thing. And I didn't spend all afternoon in your bed. It was up against the wall." She paused, reliving the afternoon in all its glory. "And on the living-room sofa." She touched her thumb to the corner of his mouth. "And we ended up in my bed. Not yours."

Beneath her thumb his lips quirked. "It was a hell of an afternoon."

"You certainly don't need my mussed hair to broadcast your sexual exploits. That smug expression on your face should do the job just fine."

She made to walk past him but he stopped her, holding on to her elbow. "I'll be as equal as you want me to be, but for tonight we're playing parts. You're the hot, slutty mistress and I'm the rich playboy so smitten with you that I've hung a fortune in jewels around your neck. Think you can handle that?"

"I can handle anything. You worry about yourself."

He chuckled softly and they continued on their way, mingling with gorgeously gowned women sparkling with diamonds. Suddenly he leaned forward and whispered in her ear. "When we get home tonight, you'll be in my bed. That's a promise."

Based on what could happen between now and then? She seriously hoped he was right.

"I was hoping to make some business contacts among these people. It is demeaning to masquerade as your hot, skanky mistress and it won't do my credibility as a businesswoman any good."

"Look at it this way. You're also being resurrected from the dead. That's got to be a reasonable trade-off."

"You are such a smart-ass. I don't know why I put up with you."

"I've been wondering the same myself for years." An older woman's rather amused voice said from behind Lexy. The voice was rich sounding, a little slow and lazy. It almost reminded her of— No. Please let the woman behind her not be—

"Lexy, darling. I'd like you to meet my mother."

Pulling every bit of backbone she could access, she turned to face Charlie's mother.

The woman gazing at her with an amusement that was eerily familiar and was astonishingly chic. She was probably in her early sixties and wore her naturally white hair in a stylish bob. Her gown was peacock-blue and brought out the blue color in her eyes and emphasized a clear complexion that she'd allowed to age naturally. Her diamond set, earrings, necklace, brooch and bracelets, was almost stunning in its brilliance.

"Mrs. Pendegraff, it's wonderful to meet you. And thank you for inviting me to this party. I've always wanted to attend."

"It's my pleasure, dear. And you must call me Sarah."

Charlie's mother extended her hand and she shook it, feeling the woman's scrutiny of her and immediately being certain she could tell what she and her son had been doing all afternoon, which naturally made her blush and feel guilty.

"May I say that in a room full of amazing jewels, your set really stands out? Those emeralds are spectacular."

"Thank you. I know I'm supposed to wear pure diamonds, but Charlie gave me this necklace so I wanted to wear it." She blushed even deeper. This was the lie they'd decided on and didn't it just figure that the first person she'd have to tell it to would be the man's mother?

Of course, if he'd told her his mother was going to be here, she'd never have agreed to the preposterous story in the first place.

"Really?" Sarah Pendcgraff shot a piercing look at her son. "How long have you two been going out together?" And the subtext was so clear she might as well have shouted it out. *And why haven't I met this girl or heard a word about her when you know her well enough to hang a fortune in jewels around her neck?*

She decided to let Charlie answer that one. This was his mother, after all.

He took her hand in his. "Be nice, Mother. You know I only introduce women to you when I'm serious. Lexy is serious."

Her hand jumped in his. He must have felt it for he squeezed her fingers reassuringly. Of course it was a lie, but for a moment her heart had done a strange bump-bump thing. Which was crazy. She didn't want to be important to Charles Pendegraff III any more than she wanted him to matter to her.

Sarah glanced searchingly between the two of them. Then smiled. "Well, I'd better get to know Lexy then, hadn't I?" She gestured to a small group standing and chatting, all of whom were fiercely elegant. Lexy knew that in the stolen jewels and a dress she couldn't possibly afford she'd fit right in, but she'd never felt more of a fraud. "Come and meet the rest of the table."

"Where's Charles II?" she asked Charlie in an undertone as they trailed his mother.

"The major British royals don't usually come unless they're in town, but we've probably got some minor royalty around."

"I meant your father."

"Ah. He passed away a few years ago."

"Oh. I'm sorry." There wasn't time for more, but she realized how very little she knew of this man who'd been inside her body. He was full of contradictions. A thief who moonlighted working for law enforcement and insurance agencies, a man who stole for a living and yet belonged to a family wealthy enough to buy a table at the Diamond Ball, a man who could be ruthless when he chose, as in when he'd grabbed and kidnapped her, who could also be a gentle and romantic lover.

Unfortunately she was a woman who loved contrasts.

She had a feeling it was safer in her jewelry designs, however, than in her choice of men.

Not that she'd chosen, really; she and Charlie had been thrown together by circumstances that were more than strange. But now that they'd been intimate, she didn't think she was going to be able to go back to her old life exactly as it was.

"My dear," Sarah Pendegraff said, drawing her forward. "I'd like you to meet some of my friends."

The friends turned out to be people she'd mostly heard of. They were either quoted in the *New York Times* business pages, or they were featured in the society pages, which she tried to keep up with for business reasons. There was so much bling in the group flashing and twinkling that she wished for sunglasses.

She shook hands all around and soon discovered she wasn't the only one who kept up with what was going on around town. "What did you say your name was?" one of the gray-haired captains of industry asked her.

"Alexandra Drake. Lexy."

His yachting-tanned forehead crinkled. "You're not the jewelry designer from SoHo, are you?"

She smiled. Resisted glancing at Charlie. Showtime, it seemed, had arrived. "Yes. That's me."

"But you're alive."

"Very much so. I was out of town when the fire broke out in my studio. I didn't hear about it until I returned."

"I believe there was a fatality involved," the man said, with a delicacy that barely masked his curiosity.

"Yes. The police are still trying to identify the woman. I don't know who she was."

"Stanley loves current events," Stanley's wife interrupted smoothly. "He'll talk your ear off if you let him. May I just say that is a stunning necklace you have there."

"Thank you." She reached for Charlie's hand in a coquettish gesture. "Charlie bought it for me."

He took her hand. Gave it a squeeze.

"My goodness." The woman who had obviously been attempting to steer the conversation into smoother channels seemed to lose her bearings. "Stanley's never given me anything half so precious." She glanced at her husband accusingly. "And they aren't even married yet."

"Do you mind if we mingle for a few minutes, Mother? I'd like to introduce Lexy to a few people."

"Of course not, dear." She glanced over his shoulder, and stopped him with a hand on his shoulder. "Oh, but before you go, you should say hello to our hosts."

Lexy's hand twitched in Charlie's as a jolt of nerves zapped her. He squeezed reassuringly, but she could feel the current of energy coming from him.

"Sarah, darling," a cultured female voice crooned. Lexy watched a woman with shoulder-length ash-blond hair and a face that belonged to a forty-year-old approach. She suspected that face would always look forty.

Apart from a waterfall of diamonds hanging from her neck, she wore a diamond tiara. Victorian era, judging by the style.

"Florence." The women air-kissed and then a man kissed Sarah's cheek in his turn. "Edward, how good it is to see you."

Edward Grayson was a dapper man of about seventy, with silver hair and red cheeks. His eyes were blue and protruded slightly behind horn-rimmed glasses.

"A lovely party, as always," Sarah continued. "I think the floral arrangements are spectacular this year."

Florence beamed. "I found this darling florist. He's from Prague, if you can imagine. He said to me, in his delightful Czech accent, 'I don't do floral arrangements, madam, I create fantasies.'"

While the women talked, Mr. Grayson smiled and nodded at the group. He got to Lexy and his smile grew rigid, his eyes bugged out and his already rosy cheeks grew scarlet. He didn't say a word, simply stood stock-still, staring at her chest. She pretended not to notice, but she felt herself beginning to blush.

"Well, it's certainly a gorgeous fantasy. Doing all the flowers in white was inspired. And the glitter on the feathers is—"

"Diamonds. They are all diamonds. Tiny industrial diamonds, he insisted on it. He had seamstresses working night and—" At this point Florence Grayson's gaze wandered and, as her husband's had, landed on Lexy's chest and stuck there.

The woman made a horrible sound in the back of her throat, like an asthmatic cat with a hair ball.

Maybe the Botox prevented her from any facial expression, but her eyes were feverish as she stared.

"Florence, are you all right?"

"Yes," the woman gasped. "Fine. The air's very dry in here." She sucked back her drink with an unsteady hand. Then tried to pull herself together.

"And how is everyone? I know you all of course, no introductions necessary, except I don't believe I've met you?" she said in a questioning tone to Lexy.

Sarah, hostess born and bred that she was, immediately introduced them. "Alexandra Drake. Charlie's friend."

"Please, call me Lexy," she said, extending her hand. She knew one thing: this woman was definitely not the same person who had come into her shop and introduced herself as Florence Grayson.

"It's lovely to meet you."

Lexy had watched carefully and while Florence Grayson hadn't reacted to hearing her name, her husband had gone rigid and, if it was possible, even redder in the face.

"Lexy Drake?" the man sputtered. "You're Lexy Drake."

"I am."

"But you're dead."

Mrs. Stanley laughed, a slick society laugh, the kind of laugh that could smooth over any awkward situation. It was getting a workout tonight. "We've already been through that, Edward. Fortunately Lexy was out of town when that awful fire happened."

"Out of town? Where?"

Charlie cleared his throat delicately. "She was with me. In a quiet, secluded not-to-be-revealed location."

"That's a lovely necklace, Lexy," Florence Grayson said, her hand reaching forward as though she were going to touch the gems, or perhaps attempt to rip them from her neck, and then drawing back.

"Isn't it gorgeous?" Mrs. Stanley gushed. "We've all been admiring it. Charlie bought it for her."

"Charlie bought it?" Mr. Grayson spoke again, his face still as red, his eyes still as buggy, as when he'd first caught sight of the necklace.

"That's right," Charlie said.

"Fine-looking piece. Where did you get it?"

"Private sale. Friend-of-a-friend sort of thing. Frankly I got it at a fire-sale price."

She had no idea how he could be so cool. All she had to do was stand here and show off the goods, but Charlie had to play a part. Cool, calculated. Giving Grayson enough information to freak him out, not enough to really tell him anything. Except for the two crucial pieces of information he was now absorbing.

Charlie had the Isabella Emeralds.

And Lexy was alive.

Grayson's gaze jerked up to Charlie's and she didn't like the expression in those protuberant blue eyes.

She had no idea what would have happened next, but luckily—or had Charlie's mother made a graceful motion?—a society photographer appeared in front of them. "May I?" He motioned with his big-lensed camera and they all dutifully arranged themselves. Charlie made sure to position Lexy at the front of the grouping so her necklace would be photographed, no doubt as yet another part of his obscure plan.

The photographer took their names and checked spellings for the photo cutline, and when he got to Lexy, paused, stared up at her and then said, "Are you the same Lexy Drake who had a fire?"

"Yes."

"That sucks. I got sent out to take the pictures. Nasty."

She nodded, feeling queasy just remembering the gutted black hole that had once been her home and business.

"Wait just a second. Didn't you die in that fire?"

"No."

He thought that over. "So, you're alive."

"As you see."

"Cool. Wait right here. There's a reporter wandering around. This could be, like, a scoop." And he tucked his notebook into his back pocket and sped off.

"Let's hope he takes good pictures," Charlie said in her ear.

"I guess it was inevitable, but I really feel strange having all this media fuss."

"Has to be done."

"I suppose. At least Amanda knows, and my dad, so they won't find out from the paper tomorrow."

Charlie turned to his mother and her friends. "If you'll all excuse us, I was about to introduce Lexy to a few people I'd like her to meet."

"Yes, of course," Grayson said, pulling himself together with an effort and finally raising his gaze from her chest. "We'll catch up with you again later."

Charlie and Lexy made their slow way through the crowd. He knew a lot of people. They hadn't gone far when a redheaded woman about Lexy's own age wearing a green strapless dress appeared, the photographer at her elbow.

"Lexy Drake?" she said. "Is it really you?"

"I'd show you my ID but I think it all melted in the fire."

"Oh, wow. This is amazing that you're alive. I was really upset when I heard the news. I've bought earrings from you before and always dreamed of being able to afford one of your custom pieces. Now I guess I can still dream."

Lexy smiled at her. She liked the woman immediately. She had freckles and a wide, innocent smile, that no doubt made people tell her all their secrets. Very handy in a journalist.

"You showing up at a charity gala very much alive is going to be news. Do you mind if I ask you a few questions?"

"No. I suppose not."

"Fantastic. First I guess I have to ask where you were and how come you didn't call anyone to say you were alive."

They'd rehearsed this story but it still felt a little awkward. Lexy didn't make a habit of distorting the truth, at least not until she got mixed up with Charlie. They'd come up with a story that was essentially true, though not entirely.

"Charlie and I were away together and—well, we didn't see or hear the news. We only returned today and I found out…"

"So you were on vacation?"

"More like a dirty weekend," Charlie put in helpfully.

Lexy glared at him. She really didn't need that being printed in the newspaper.

"This must be a huge shock for you. How did it feel when you got back to find out your studio was gone?"

"It's like a part of me died," she said, recalling the sick feeling she'd experienced when she drove by.

"I hate to ask you this, but it's my job. Do you know there was a body found in the rubble?"

"I heard that, yes."

"Any idea who it could be?"

"No. The police are investigating and of course I'll help in any way I can."

"It's strange to see you in public and not wearing one of your own designs, but I have to say this is a truly stunning piece."

"Thank you. Charlie gave it to me. It's especially precious to me now that I have no jewelry of my own to wear. Though, of course, I'll get back to work as soon as I can find a new space. And, if it's possible, could you please print that I will honor all of my orders and commissions. I'll put something on my Web site so customers can get hold of me."

"Of course. So how does it feel to discover everyone thought you were dead?"

Lexy thought about it for a moment. Her mind darting to the activities of the afternoon. "I'd have to say, I've never felt more alive."

"I'm really happy you are." She turned to the photographer. "Can you get a picture of Lexy and her boyfriend?"

"Sure, yeah."

"Do a great job. I think we're looking at our front page," the woman said with all the satisfaction of a society reporter who just stumbled on a front-page news headline.

He snapped off a few photographs of Charlie and Lexy standing together.

After the photo session, Charlie whisked her away and toward the opposite side of the room. "How are you doing?" he asked in a low voice, a caressing smile on his face presumably to convince anyone watching that they were exchanging sweet nothings.

She pasted a matching smile on her own lips. "I'm

sweating in places I didn't know I had sweat glands," she said.

"You're doing great," he said, leaning forward and giving her a little kiss. Which definitely helped steady her.

"Security guards closing in," she whispered against his lips. "Three o'clock."

He smiled, as though he were quite happy about this turn of events. She supposed they'd provoked Grayson hoping for some reaction, but right now she really wished she were curled in bed in her pajamas with a good book.

"Let's dance," he said, not bothering to look over his shoulder and confirm what she'd seen.

The game of cat-and-mouse had begun.

The gala was packed. Due to the high net worth of everybody here, except her, the age range was predictably on the upper end, but there were some younger celebrities, up-and-coming hotshot business types and trophy wives and dates to balance things out.

When they got to the dance floor, the live orchestra was playing a waltz, which she probably hadn't danced since the last time she attended a wedding. But she loved dancing, and when Charlie pulled her into his arms, she had no trouble following his moves.

As their bodies touched and brushed she found her mind filling with images of their sex games earlier and in spite of the nervous tension she was experiencing, or maybe because of it, her senses seemed heightened. She felt the brush of his wool jacket against her bare arms, the heat of his body where they touched, the subtle movements of his hips and legs, his arms guiding her as they swooped in circles around the dance floor. She didn't need to keep him informed of the location of the two goons dressed as security guards, since he could see them for himself.

She tried not to stare, but it was impossible not to stay aware of them as they watched from the edges of the dance floor, waiting.

When the second security guard turned and stared directly at her, she stumbled slightly.

In that second she was back at the night her place was broken into and later torched. She remembered clearly staring out of the limo window and seeing the guy running, a gun held in his hand.

"You all right?" Charlie asked, smoothly guiding her back into the dance.

All right? She'd never been less all right. Her heart was hammering and she felt her breath hitch. "The second security guard? I recognize him."

"Shh. I know."

"You saw him, too? It's the one from that night. The one who ran out after us the night my place was torched."

He winced as she accidentally stepped on his toe but she barely noticed.

"The guys who were pretending to be cops. You were right. They were hired by Grayson. But imagine the nerve, having them here tonight."

"Remember, they have no idea that you saw them. And they couldn't connect me with any of this until tonight."

"We should call my dad right now. He can arrest that guy."

"On what charge?" The song ended and they clapped politely along with the other dancers. A few left the floor, more joined them.

"How about murder? Arson? Impersonating an officer?"

"Did you actually see him do any of those things?"

She opened her mouth. Closed it again. Damn. A few reruns of *Law & Order* would tell her she had no case. Never mind years of living in the same house as a cop. Her excitement fizzled. "Nope. All I saw him do was run down a street with a gun in his hand."

"It's not enough. The only thing we have going for us is that they have no idea how much we know. Let's keep it that way for a while."

"I wish they'd stop staring at us. It's creeping me out."

"Relax. They won't do anything here—not with my mother, your father and half the power players in the city watching."

She knew he was right, theoretically, but she couldn't rid her mind of the image of that brutish guy with the short neck running along her street with a gun. What if he'd caught up with them?

She remembered the news report about the body in her apartment and she knew the answer.

They left the dance floor and he scooped them two champagne flutes from a passing tray and handed her one. She needed the false courage, so she sipped the dry, bubbly wine on the theory that it was hard to take anything too seriously when champagne was involved.

Charlie introduced her to a few more people he knew, as though this were a normal social event. Then it was time for dinner.

No doubt the most fabulous, delicious dinner ever created. It might as well have been boxed mac and cheese for all she could taste.

She couldn't stop noticing that she was always

watched. She worked out that there were four of them, paired off so that one team would keep her and Charlie in their sights and then they'd trade off. As though she might not notice the surveillance if it was always a different thick-necked type in a bad suit eyeing her.

There were speeches, of course, more dancing, more mingling. Charlie seemed the epitome of relaxed charm. He laughed, he joked, he ate with the apparent relish of a man who could actually taste his food. She wanted to hit him.

Once the speeches were over and people had begun to circulate, the event she'd been dreading occurred. Mr. Grayson approached, without his wife.

He was all smiles as he patted Charlie on the back all hail fellow well met. She could almost feel his eyeballs longing to stray to her neckline, but he controlled himself with an effort.

"Charles, I've got something to discuss that I think you might find interesting."

"Really?" Charlie managed to combine surprise with flattery in his tone to a degree that would have impressed Stanislavski.

"If you can spare me a few minutes in my study, there's something I'd like to show you."

"Of course." He turned to Lexy with a smile and the ghost of a wink. "All right if I leave you for a few minutes, darling?"

Before she could reply, Grayson said, "Come along with us, Ms. Drake. I'd value your expertise."

"All right."

He led them to a private elevator in a corner and they rode it up two floors. She knew he couldn't do anything violent to them, not during the gala and certainly not with Charlie's mother downstairs, but still she felt her anxiety ratchet up a notch. She had to restrain her fingers from floating to her necklace and toying with it nervously. She gripped her clutch bag instead, squeezing and releasing the poor thing as though it were a stress ball.

The elevator opened on the quiet hush of a well-insulated home. No noise from the party penetrated. She hadn't realized how noisy it was downstairs until she felt the heavy quality of the silence.

"I keep my offices up here. I do most of my work from home, these days. Much less exhausting."

The hallway was lushly carpeted so her heels were soundless. He punched a code on a heavy door, which opened on a luxurious office, like something out of a men's club. Deep maroon leather club chairs, a desk big enough for a king to run a country from.

A second desk held several top-of-the-line computers, but the desk Grayson eased himself behind was bare of clutter, either technological or paper based. Somehow she found the gleaming bare surface kind of creepy.

In a gesture so clichéd she could barely believe he did it, he went to a cabinet and pulled out a humidor. Offered it to Charlie. "Cigar?"

Charlie chose a Cuban.

Grayson chose one for himself and soon the two men were puffing, adding a fog of sweet-scented smoke to her already addled brain.

Grayson didn't waste any time in getting to the point.

"I couldn't help but admire your necklace, my dear."

Now, at last, she allowed her fingers to touch the sparkling confection at her chest. "Isn't it something? Charlie bought it for me."

"Which brings us to the point of this little chat," the man said smoothly, his gaze still locked on the emeralds and diamonds. "Of course, discretion is assured, but I must tell you that I recently was burgled and a necklace identical to that one went missing."

Charlie raised his eyebrows. She felt equally surprised. She hadn't imagined the man would honestly tell them the jewels belonged to him. "Really? That's quite a coincidence."

A small smile that looked somehow dangerous appeared on the aging cherub's face. "I don't believe in coincidence. In my experience there's usually a logical explanation."

And she knew exactly what the explanation was. She couldn't believe he could act so cool.

Charlie didn't speak, merely puffed his cigar, leaning back in his chair as though he had nothing to do and all evening to do it in.

Grayson said, "Who sold you the piece?"

"Sorry. It was a private sale. As I said, an old friend needed some quick cash and I liked the look of the piece."

"You've got a good eye. What did you pay for it?"

A low chuckle was his answer. "It was a gift for Lexy. I don't want her knowing how much I paid."

The smile was growing thinner by the moment. "Ms. Drake, you're a jeweler. What's your estimate of the value of the piece you're wearing?"

She paused, as though she'd never considered anything so vulgar as value. She glanced down at the sparkling stones winking up at her.

"I'd estimate that a collection of emeralds and diamonds of this size and quality would run close to a million dollars."

"That's a pretty good guess, my dear. To me, of course, there's the added sentimental value. That necklace holds fond memories."

"Forgive me," said Charlie, "but I don't ever recall seeing it before. Surely if your wife had worn it I'd have noticed. I've a good memory for jewelry. That's one of the reasons I bought this piece. It was unique."

"You're right. As I said, it's got sentimental value and also I've kept it very private."

"Well, I guess there's more than one of them around after all. I assure you, the person who sold this to me is no thief."

Grayson's fingers tapped his immaculate desk surface sounding like machine-gun fire.

"I'm sure your insurers will be able to compensate you for the loss if the police don't have any luck locating your property." Charlie blew a few smoke rings.

"Well, that's the problem right there. I never insured the piece. As you've noted, my wife never wore it, and I thought I had it safe. Somehow, it was discovered and stolen."

"Odd that your wife's truly stunning collection of diamonds that she's wearing this evening weren't also taken."

"Yes. That was a lucky thing." Grayson opened a desk drawer and drew out a bank ledger. Old-fashioned and somehow commanding. "Let me get right to the point. I'd like to buy the necklace from you. Never mind what you paid. If we take Lexy's rough evaluation and add, let's say another half a million for your time and trouble, shall we say a million and a half?"

"You want to buy my necklace?" Lexy said, doing her best to appear astonished and hurt. "But I couldn't part with it. It was Charlie's first real gift to me."

"With a million and a half, I'm sure *Charlie* could buy you something more useful. An apartment perhaps. I believe you are currently homeless, Ms. Drake."

An apartment was not the most tactful item to bring up since he must know that she'd been burned out of her last home thanks to him. A shiver ran over her skin as she thought how truly deadly this old choir boy was.

Charlie looked perfectly unconcerned. "Up to you, babe. The necklace is yours." Like the most useless playboy bazillionaire, as though a million here or there didn't really bother him so long as it didn't make him late for his polo match.

"I'm sorry, Mr. Grayson. I've had so many compliments on my necklace tonight I'd hate to part with it. Besides, I'm not the kind of girl who sells presents somebody bought her." She shot Charlie a particularly intimate smile. "Particularly not somebody really special."

Grayson hadn't become a bazillionaire himself by wasting his time. It was obvious she wasn't going to change her mind, so he put the ledger carefully back in his drawer. She had a moment when she wondered whether he'd pull out a gun next and force her to give up the goods but as Charlie had predicted, he couldn't do that, not with the party going on downstairs. Not when half the people there had complimented Lexy on her fine necklace.

"Well, my dear, if you ever change your mind and decide to sell, do let me know. It's astonishingly like the one I lost."

"I will. And I hope you find yours." What she really meant was, *I hope you get yours.*

"Let's go back and join the party, shall we?"

The men put out their cigars and the three of them

retraced their quiet steps, whooshed down in the elevator and rejoined the gala.

"And the curtain closes on Act One," Charlie said softly.

19

THE LINE OF LIMOS stretched as the guests made their way home at the end of the evening. Lexy caught her father, one of the cops on the detail, and he looked visibly relieved when he saw her and Charlie get into their limo, driven, of course, by Healey.

"They following?" Charlie asked as they pulled away and headed toward the hotel.

"Yep."

"You know what to do."

"Sure do." Healey shot a glance at the pair of them. "Be careful."

The limo dropped them at the hotel and after the doorman helped Lexy out, followed by Charlie, it pulled away.

They walked into the hotel lobby. Charlie checked for messages. There were none.

They rode the elevator up to their floor. Entered their suite. Charlie flipped on lights. Came up behind her.

He kissed the back of her neck, making her shiver. "I'd love to peel you out of these clothes and make love to you right now, but honey, we've got to move."

She nodded. They'd rehearsed this part already.

He unfastened the necklace, placed it carefully in a plain black jewelry case. Then he opened the original Isabella Emeralds box where an identical necklace lay. The one Lexy and Amanda had sweated over. "You did an amazing job."

"Let's hope I didn't waste my time and your money."

He put the box into the in-room safe, locking it carefully. Then he and Lexy stripped out of their clothes and slipped into their waiting jeans and sweaters. She was thankful for her new boots and the coat. She wrapped the scarf around her throat. Gloves would have been nice but she didn't have any. It couldn't be helped.

She took their discarded evening clothes and scattered them in a seductive trail toward one of the bedrooms while he took pillows and made two vaguely human-size sausages in the middle of the bed.

Within ten minutes they'd turned out the lights and exited the suite. He was carrying a black leather bag. She didn't even ask. Moving swiftly to the stairs, they ran lightly down, and down, and down.

She was out of breath by the time they'd scooted out a back door and headed to where a slick, powerful-looking black motorcycle waited.

He unzipped the black bag and pulled out a helmet. "You ever ridden on one of these?"

She grinned at him. "All around Europe. The summer of my Italian boyfriend."

He tossed her the helmet. Also black. "You're experienced, then."

"Oh, yeah." She put the helmet on, tucking her hair underneath. Charlie put his own helmet on and then climbed onto the bike. She swung a leg over and snugged up behind him on the pillion, settling into a posture she remembered well.

They roared off into the night. Even though she had her arms wrapped around Charlie's waist, her hands still quickly chilled against the cool night air. It was three in the morning and New York was still busy with cabs, emergency vehicles and garbage trucks.

She had no idea where they were going and it was typical of this bizarre adventure that she hadn't bothered to ask. She knew Charlie had a plan, had thrown him her trust as easily as he'd thrown her the bike helmet. Maybe it was crazy, but ever since he'd entered her studio mere days ago, her life had been nothing but insane.

If the adventure ended well, and she really, really hoped it did, there'd be no reason for them to stay together. She wasn't the kind of woman men showered with million-dollar necklaces. She never aspired to wear the big-ticket bling; she'd always appreciated individual design rather than the number of karats something represented. Style over dollar value.

She didn't belong in Charlie's world any more than she belonged at that fancy gala tonight. Still, it had been fun playing Cinderella at the ball. Now, her dress had turned into jeans, her limo into a motorbike and her fancy necklace into evidence to catch a murderer.

That was the plan, anyway. But plans, as she knew well, didn't always go, well, according to plan.

The motorcycle dipped as he took turns fast and she stayed with him, leaning into his body, letting the bike do its thing. She didn't fight the movement, so the three of them—bike, Charlie and her—moved as one.

The adrenaline was still pumping through her system and somehow a ride through the night was perfect.

He slowed, pulled out a pass and brought it to a

sensor; then a gate opened and they sped through into a garage. He parked and they dismounted.

"Where are we?" she asked.

"My place." He kissed her swiftly. "I promised you I was going to make love to you in my bed."

He walked to an elevator. He needed to punch in a code to use it, she noted. Pretty good security in this building. The elevator took them straight to the top floor and then opened into a small foyer with only one door.

Another code, and a finger scan, and then the door opened.

"Cool," she said and walked inside.

And her mouth fell open. It was like walking into an interior designer's vision of what Lexy had always secretly dreamed of. The apartment was huge, with high ceilings, open beams, a circular staircase to a second level.

The walls were decorated with bold, original art. She walked straight to the window and looked out on the river.

"This is amazing."

"Thanks."

"You took me to a hotel when you have this?" She waved her arm around the apartment.

"Didn't know you well enough."

"Now you do?"

He walked toward her, put a hand to the back of her head, pulled her forward for a kiss. "Now, I do."

His cell phone rang. He answered, "Yeah, Healey." Checked his watch and nodded. "Right on time. No. Let Jed know, make sure you follow them."

"Yeah. I will."

He ended the call. Turned to her. "Dumbass One and Dumbass Two just entered the hotel."

She let out a breath she hadn't realized she was holding. "Grayson took the bait."

"Yep. Now let's hope those boys can manage to break in to the safe and steal the emeralds." He sighed and rubbed the back of his neck. "Maybe we made it too difficult for them putting the jewels in the safe. I should have left them out on the bureau."

"We talked about this," she reminded him. "If we made it too easy he might sense a trap. I'm sure they'll figure out a way to get into that safe."

"And lead us straight to Papa."

Charlie withdrew a flat box from inside his leather coat. Opened it carefully.

"How'd they survive the trip?" She peeked over his shoulder. The Isabella Emeralds winked at her.

"I guess they've survived shipwrecks, airline travel and who knows what else in five centuries. A motorcycle ride wasn't going to bother them."

She touched a deep green emerald with her fingertip. "I wonder how long it will take him to spot the fake."

"Initially he'll see what he wants to see. His necklace. We have the element of surprise on our side, plus his own greed and mania working against him. A man who would be willing to kill three people to keep those gems all to himself couldn't be too sane."

"No. Which only makes him more dangerous."

"I agree. So we play it safe. Your part in this little drama is over."

She wasn't going to argue with the man at this time of the morning, but she really didn't think her part was over. Not yet.

"I know that necklace wasn't the real Isabella one,

but even so, you put out a lot of money buying real stones."

He shrugged. "The man tried to kill me and you. I have a vested interest in taking him down."

"I just hope the tracking device is hidden well enough. If I'd had more time, I'd have done a better job."

"Honey, you are way too much of a perfectionist. I swear when I first looked at them side by side, I couldn't tell the difference. Besides, we don't want him believing he's got the real gems or we'll never get him. He's got to figure out we conned him."

"That's twice now he's tried to get the necklace back and failed. He seems like the kind of guy who's going to be very unhappy when he figures that out."

"And I hope I'm around to see it." He took her arm in his. "Let's go track our package."

She ought to be dead tired, but she still felt wired, so she followed him to his office on the upper level. She wasn't really surprised to see another set of security measures before the heavy door opened and she entered a large office with enough equipment to run NATO.

"Have a seat," he said, pulling out a high-tech office chair and pulling it next to a similar chair that sat in front of a large-screen monitor. He fired up the computer, typed in a few commands and chuckled. "There it is. On the move."

It was amazingly cool to watch the blip that was the GPS tracking device making its way through a computerized street map. As they'd hoped, it was headed toward the Grayson mansion.

"I guess they figured out how to break in to the safe after all."

"Guess so."

"You sound awfully pleased with yourself."

"I am." He gripped her thigh in a warm clasp. "We did it. He swallowed the bait."

They watched until the blip stopped moving. "Do you suppose it's in his safe?"

"Or under his pillow. I doubt he's going to put it around his next mistress's neck."

She shuddered. "When do you think he'll figure out it's not the original?"

"If he's the fanatical collector I think he is, he's going to have an expert verify that it's unharmed. That's when he'll figure it out. If we're lucky, that will be tomorrow."

"What if he doesn't call anyone in?"

"Then we call the cops. Tell them about the break-in and about the lucky security measures we took to protect the necklace. They'll track the stolen goods to Grayson."

They watched the stationary blip for a few more minutes. "Well, looks like the action's over for tonight." He glanced at her. "Ready for bed?"

She nodded.

"Tired?" The skin around his eyes crinkled and just the tips of his lips tilted up. It was one of the sexiest things she'd ever seen.

Slowly she shook her head.

He spun her chair so they were facing each other. "So, you want to go to bed, but you're not tired?"

"That's right."

He leaned over, cupping her face with his palm, reaching around to the back of her head and unfastening her hair so it tumbled, glossy and dark, bouncing around her shoulders. "I do like your hair," he said, sifting the strands through his fingers.

"Thanks."

"Know what else I like?"

She shook her head.

"A little something called the Lyons Stagecoach."

She clapped her hands over her eyes. "A gentleman would never bring that up."

He was laughing as he pulled her hands away and kissed her fingers. "A gentleman always tries to give a lady what she wants."

Half embarrassed, half turned on, she followed him as he led her to his big, gorgeous bed. He undressed her slowly, as though her jeans and sweater were a fancy evening gown, then he stripped off his own clothes.

She was so hot for him she couldn't believe they'd had sex most of the afternoon.

He pushed her back onto the bed and they rolled and played, naked and silly. The relief that everything was going according to plan was enormous. He kissed her, touched her everywhere, then sitting in the middle of the bed, he pulled her onto his lap, her knees on either side of his hips. While they kissed, he reached down and began to play with her, getting her hot and juicy. She climbed onto him, easing him into her body, then leaned back on her hands; he leaned back on his and they started to rock the stagecoach.

"Why do you like it so much?" he asked, half panting.

"I like the slide, the way you hit my G-spot, the amount of control I have."

"I like the view," he said, grinning.

Excitement was building, building, she could hear them both panting, and then her head fell back, her hair cascaded down her back and she came in a great swamp of feeling. Seconds later she heard his cry of release.

She leaned forward, slumped on top of him, knocking him onto his back, falling with him.

"Is it really your favorite?" he asked when they could speak again.

She kissed his chest. "It's right up there." But then so was everything else they'd done. "I'm glad you knew," she murmured drowsily.

He kissed her hair. "Me, too."

20

"GOOD MORNING."

Charlie turned from contemplation of the morning paper to see Lexy wrapped in his robe. Her hair was a glorious mess, mostly because he'd had his hands in it so often in the night, and then she'd done some mussing of her own, he recalled, thrashing her head back and forth on the pillow.

"Good morning."

Her skin looked extra pale against the navy silk of the robe, and its size made her appear particularly dainty. Her bare feet were long and he loved the dark purple color on her toenails.

"Want some breakfast?"

She stifled a yawn with the back of her hand. "Coffee?"

"Fresh pot."

"Heaven." But she didn't head straight for the kitchen; she came toward him and gave him a quick kiss. "Did we get any sleep last night?"

He grinned. "Not much."

Stifling her own smile and another yawn, she headed for the kitchen. "Time is it?"

"After eleven."

He'd thought about waking her earlier, but she'd been sleeping like a woman who needed the sleep. He folded the paper, watched her sip coffee the way a vampire might suck blood, greedily, as though her very life depended on it.

"I need to run back to the hotel and discover the break-in. You want to come or hang out here?"

She looked startled. "You'd trust me here alone? What if I pushed the wrong button in mission control up there and started a war?"

"Of course I trust you. I'll even tell you the good places to snoop."

She snorted. "Please. You're not that interesting. Anyhow, I want to come with you. We'll discover the break-in together."

He pushed the now-closed paper toward her. "You're front-page news."

"Oh, right. I forgot."

She wandered over and looked down at the photo. "'Missing Jeweler Turns Up Alive At Diamond Ball.' Not the most imaginative headline." She tilted her head. "Good picture, though. And that necklace really photographs well. No need to describe the missing piece of jewelry. We can simply point to today's paper." She glanced up at him admiringly. "Nice."

"Grayson is going to have a cow."

"That thought makes me very happy. Let me grab a shower and dress. I'll be ready in twenty."

"Want some toast or something?"

She was already sprinting up the stairs. "Sure. Anything."

He had to give her credit. She was one of the few women he could think of who could actually shower and dress in twenty minutes. Impressive. One more attribute in a growing list of things he adored about this woman. Not the least was the way she gave her body with absolute joy and abandon.

"What's that weird smile about?" she asked as she came down the last couple of stairs eighteen minutes after she'd gone up them.

"I was thinking about last night. You are very flexible."

She grinned at him. "Yoga. And pole dancing."

He offered her the whole-grain toast and peanut butter he'd made her. "Pole dancing?"

"Okay. Mostly yoga. But I did take pole dancing once. It's harder than it looks. Takes a lot of arm strength."

"You never stop surprising me."

They were still teasing each other when they arrived back at the hotel. Since they knew the jewels were gone he couldn't think of any reason for Grayson's thugs to be waiting in their room, but still he called Healey to meet them and made Lexy wait while he and Healey entered the room first.

A five-second run-through told them there was no one in the suite but them, so he motioned Lexy inside.

"Oh, my God. Why would they make such a mess?" she asked, surveying the damage.

"Could be to make it look like a real robbery," Healey suggested. "They had to trash your stuff looking for money and stuff. Then hit the safe."

The door of the safe swung wide, the empty gray metal box bereft of its contents.

"Wow. I hardly had anything, just a few new things,

now it's all ruined. Again." She sounded upset. He and Healey exchanged a glance.

"Don't touch anything."

"I won't."

She walked toward one bedroom, obviously forcing herself not to pick up the belongings that were scattered on the floor. The sexy trail of last night's clothes mixed with tossed cushions and broken cosmetics. She entered the bedroom and made a strange, choking sound.

"Lexy?" She didn't answer. Her back was stiff and she seemed rooted to a spot just inside the doorway.

"Lex? You okay?"

"I think…" she began in a strange, high-pitched tone not at all like herself. "I think…"

He didn't wait for more. He sprinted to her side. "Babe, what is it?"

She pointed a trembling finger to the bed. "I think those are bullet holes."

"Holy shit." The quick sausagelike mounds he'd made in the bed to fool any intruders into thinking they were asleep now sported charred holes. He put an arm around Lexy and pulled her to his side. "Healey, you'd better see this."

Healey joined them. He stepped closer to the bed. "From the size of those holes, looks like a .38, maybe a 9 mm. Must have used a silencer." He regarded them with hard eyes. "Grayson sure wants you two dead."

"I'm starting to feel the same way about him."

He pulled Lexy gently from the room. Her face was pale and she was trembling lightly. Shock. She'd been amazing, shouldering the strain of the past few days, but this was one bad experience too many. He sat her down on a chair. Got to his knees before her and rubbed her hands. "It's okay. It's going to be okay. I won't let anyone hurt you. I promise." Over his shoulder he said to Healey, "Make the calls."

"Sorry." She blinked a few times as though clearing her eyes of a gruesome sight. "I'm not going to fall apart, I promise. That just… What if we'd…"

"Shh. We didn't. He won't get another chance."

She nodded.

The police and hotel security arrived about the same time. And for the next half hour they went through their story. Ballistics experts were brought in, a photographer, fingerprint guys, a pair of detectives. Which impressed Charlie until he realized the bullet holes upped a theft charge to attempted murder.

His mind flipped to what could have happened and a cold, ruthless anger began to surge inside him.

Lexy's dad was through the door in seconds, out of breath and red in the face. He took one look at his daughter's pale expression and jogged to her side. "What happened here?"

He didn't coddle her, Charlie noticed. Probably never had, but his concern was evident in every cell of his belligerent body.

"The break-in went exactly as we hoped. With one added detail." He didn't like looking up at Jed Dabrowski when he had this kind of news to deliver, so he gave Lexy's fingers a quick squeeze and rose. "They shot up the bedding we'd rolled up to make it look like we were sleeping."

It hadn't occurred to him until the words were out that he was admitting to a very irate father who happened to carry a gun for a living that he was sleeping with his only daughter. Also, putting her life in danger. From Jed's expression, he'd just made himself number one on the shit list.

"Show me."

He led him into the room, crawling with photographers and the fingerprint experts while a security guy from the hotel stood there seeming not to know what to do.

"Detective," Jed said, nodding to a man in plainclothes about his own age who was studying the bed.

"Sergeant."

"So, what do you think?"

It seemed like they knew each other, probably respected each other's abilities because the detective said, "Six shots fired, probably from the doorway."

"Somebody wanted those two real dead. Obviously the perp thought these two were sleeping."

"Or did they? Maybe they knew they were shooting into pillows." The detective sighed, walking out of the room and motioning Jed and Charlie to follow. Removed his latex gloves when he got to the outer room. "Problem is, even if we find the guys who did the shooting all they have to say is that they knew there was nobody in the bed. It was a warning. Target practice. They can say anything they want. If they claim they knew there was nobody in that bed, we can't get them on attempted murder."

Jed stalked back over to his daughter. She was looking better now, Charlie was glad to see. Her color was back and she seemed steadier. He was pretty sure her dad was going to try to bully her into going home to his place. He was about to go on over there and explain why that was a terrible idea. His place was as close to impregnable as he could make it.

She needed to stay with him. He looked across at her, her dainty features, the long dark hair he loved to push his hands through, the lithe body that made magic with his. He needed to protect her.

As though she sensed his scrutiny, she glanced up at him and smiled. And that was when it hit him.

He was in love with her.

Perfect. In the middle of a crisis, when their lives were in danger and a madman was after them, now he had to fall in love?

Well, he'd never made things easy on himself. Why would he start now?

He took a step toward Lexy and her dad, feeling suddenly awkward with this new knowledge. Felt good, though. Right.

His phone rang. His mother.

"Hi, Mom."

"Hello, sweetheart. How are you?"

Well, if he couldn't tell his mom, who could he tell? "I'm in love."

She laughed softly. "I know that, dear. I saw you look at her last night." She sighed. "It's how your father used to look at me."

"I remember." He did, too. They fought, his mom and dad, they weren't the bloodless "everything's fine" types that so many of his friends' parents were. His were passionate people. Not demonstrative in public, but sometimes he'd catch his dad planting a good one on his mom, or she'd pat his dad's butt in passing. Stupid little things, but they'd always made him feel good as a kid. "I wish Dad was around. I wouldn't mind his advice."

"I know." She cleared her throat. "I was actually calling to speak with Lexy. Is she there?"

"What do you want to talk to Lexy for?" He was standing in front of her now, and she raised her eyebrows at his words. He mouthed, "My mother." At the words, his brand-new love looked startled and mildly panicked.

"Never you mind. If she had a phone I'd have called her directly. Put her on, please."

It was a tone he'd never yet been able to argue against. He was a grown man but he doubted he ever would be able to hold out against that particular tone of command.

With a shrug, he handed his phone over.

Lexy ran her tongue over her lips and took a quick breath before saying, "Hello?"

She listened for a moment.

"Oh, lunch. Today. Well, that's very nice of you, but—"

"Of course. Yes, a late lunch is fine. Two o'clock." She sent an S.O.S. with her eyes. "Yes, that's perfect."

She flipped the phone shut. Turned a stunned face to his. "How does she do that? I was going to say no, and then she said, 'I'd really love it if you could make it today,' and suddenly I'm saying yes.'"

"I know. It's the tone. My mother could rule the world. It's very scary."

"But why does she want to have lunch with me?"

"Probably to tell you how much she wants grand-children."

"Sounds like a sensible woman," Jed chimed in. "Lunch with a nice woman would do you good." He turned to Charlie. "How's the security at your mother's?"

"Adequate. But don't worry. I'll be there."

Lexy handed him back his phone. "Um, you're not invited."

"I know. I'll keep an eye on the house. Until this thing is over, I'm not letting you out of my sight."

She looked as though she were going to argue, but her father nodded in approval. "If she won't come home with me, I guess you're the next best choice."

He nodded. "Jed, can I talk to you privately for a second?"

Lexy bristled at that. "What? What could you possibly want to talk to my father about that I couldn't hear?"

"I'm going to ask his permission to marry you."

"Oh, very funny. Ha-ha. Okay, don't tell me. Have your little guy talk and I'll sit here and look pretty. If anyone needs a sandwich or a foot rub or something, just let me know."

The two men stepped outside into the hallway.

"Well?" Jed asked. "Something you need to tell me?"

Now that the moment had arrived Charlie felt stupidly nervous. He'd imagined this moment would come someday, that he and the father of his intended would enjoy a brandy and a cigar in comfort while he laid out his plans for the future and formally asked to marry the man's daughter. Sure, it was old-fashioned, but it was what his father would have expected of him.

But there was no brandy to sip in a bid to steady his nerves, no cigar to puff and avoid speaking for a second or two. It was him, a guy who had every reason to hate his guts since he'd endangered his only daughter, and a security guard down by the elevator looking at them curiously.

"Look, I know my timing pretty much sucks, but I want something out in the open."

Jed crossed his arms over his ample belly. "You're sleeping with my daughter. I got eyes. I figured it out.

You should know I'm not some modern-type father. You hurt her and I kill you. Simple as that."

"I love her, Jed."

"Words are cheap. I'm not impressed."

He blew out a breath. "You're not going to be one of those easygoing fathers-in-law, are you?"

For the first time the pugnacious expression disappeared from Jed's face. "Father-in-law? Did you say father-in-law?"

"That's right. I'm bungling this badly, I know, but I really did want to ask your permission to marry your daughter."

A deep chuckle resonated from the man standing in front of him. "She doesn't know anything about this, does she?"

"No. I know it's all moving pretty fast, but I'm thirty-four years old. I've never been in love before, never wanted to marry anyone before. Now, I can't imagine my life without Lexy. I want to live with her and love her and have children with her. And I'd like your permission before I ask her."

Jed rocked back on his heels, every inch the cop. "Well, this is an interesting situation." He chuckled. "Gotta tell you, not one I ever thought I'd find myself in. Lexy, she's not the kind of girl who believes in stuff like this. She's modern. But not me. I think you did fine." He scratched at the back of his head. "So, before I give my permission, I guess there's some things I should ask you. Let's see. I know she's a successful business gal, but she's taken quite a hit recently. You gonna be able to provide for her?"

"Yes. Money's really not a problem. I've got a very high net worth."

"Look, Charlie, no offense, but I got no time for

hedge funds and collections of old brandy and fancy cars. I'm a simple man. You got money in the bank? A house? Real assets?"

"I own quite a bit of property. All mortgage free. And I can have my accountant go over my other assets. Trust me, Lexy will only work because she wants to."

"Okay. Are you a gambler? A drinking man?"

"Only moderately."

"Ever been in trouble with the law?"

Damn it. He supposed he'd always known it would come out. But he'd hoped there'd be a better time. "Not exactly. But I should tell you something you won't like." Of all the men he could be having this conversation with, a cop wouldn't be his first choice. "I've never exactly had trouble with the law, but I have to tell you the truth. I used to be a thief."

"Come again?"

"I was a thief. A pretty good one, too. Never caught."

He shrugged. "I guess I was bored. Didn't want to go into my father's law firm, and I figured the financial industry was full of crooks. I decided it was more honest to be an actual crook than one who wears a suit to the office every day."

"That's a puny justification for breaking the law."

"I know. If it's any consolation, I only stole from people who could afford to lose things. Now I've turned my talents to an honest business. I work to get stolen goods back. Kind of a nice switch."

A noncommittal grunt was his only reply.

They stood there in the hallway for an uncomfortable minute. He supposed he'd imagined the asking-for-permission thing would be a quick run-through for

form's sake. It had never honestly occurred to him that
Jed Dabrowski might turn him down.

Then he'd be stuck in a nice dilemma. He wasn't
going to give up Lexy, not because her father said so.
As it was he had no idea if his feelings were returned.
Did she love him?

They'd known each other such a short time. Intense,
but short. Obviously they had incendiary passion between them, and they seemed to get on well together,
which had to be a miracle considering the stress load
they'd been under since the beginning. For him, the
pressure cooker of tension and passion had turned to
love. For Lexy? He had no idea. Maybe she'd walk away
from him the second Grayson was in police custody and
this adventure was over. Which would be soon.

The thought of that happening was too painful to
contemplate. If she didn't love him now, he could wait.
He'd give her time, let her rebuild, be the supportive
boyfriend. Friend even if that was all she'd give him.
But he wouldn't give up.

Finally his hopefully future father-in-law spoke. "I
spent my whole career enforcing the law. I'm not happy
about what you've told me. But you were man enough
to come clean, and I appreciate that. I'm not saying
yes, I approve of you marrying my daughter, and I'm
not saying no. I think we all need to slow down a little.
Ask me again in a month."

Okay, so it wasn't the pat on the back and fatherly approval he'd hoped for. It wasn't cuffs and getting shoved
in the back of the paddy wagon, either. All in all, he
figured Jed had handled the news pretty well. "Thank
you, sir." He stuck out his hand and this time Lexy's dad
shook it.

The door to the suite opened and Lexy swept out. "What are you two doing out here?"

"Man talk, young lady. None of your business."

"You and your man talk." She grabbed Charlie's arm. "I need to go shopping again. I can't wear jeans to your mother's for lunch."

She could and his mother wouldn't care, but he understood there were deep-seated female rituals he knew nothing about, just as Lexy would no doubt never comprehend why he'd felt compelled to ask her father for her hand in marriage.

Or that he respected the cop more for bluntly telling him he needed to prove himself worthy than he'd have felt if the man had been all smiles and "welcome to the family."

They said their goodbyes and then he and Lexy headed out of the hotel.

"If I ever get a day when people aren't trying to kill me, I really need to get to my bank and get new cards and checks and things. It's so weird not even having a debit card so I can use the ATM."

"I know. I feel terrible about all the trouble I've cost you." He put an arm around her. "So, get your revenge. Go ahead and max out my platinum card."

She sent him a taunting look. "Don't tempt me. We're on Fifth Avenue and I have very good taste."

He took that moment to kiss her, finding her lips soft and full. He felt them curve beneath his as his arms came around her and a little kiss turned into something much more.

"Yep," he said, pulling away, "Definitely good taste."

21

WHEN THEY DREW UP at the gates of Charlie's mother's mansion she realized that Charlie's family was even richer than she'd realized. The place was one of those huge old mansions built in the boom times of lumber magnates, railway barons and oil tycoons.

He drove her about two hundred miles up a tree-lined driveway to the mansion. "Don't worry," he said, when she hesitated to get out of the car. "You'll be fine."

She drew in a breath. Nodded. Put her hand on the door handle.

As she was getting out of the car, he said, "By the way, I love you."

She stuck her head back in and stared at him. "What did you say?"

His eyes laughed up at her, but she saw the earnestness behind them. "I said, I love you."

"And you tell me now?"

"I figure it will take your mind off being scared of my mother."

Her hand went to her heart. She searched his face for a "gotcha" sign, but there wasn't one. If anything he appeared uncertain for the first time since she'd met him.

"You're serious," she whispered.

"Yeah."

"But—"

"No buts. My ego can't take them right now. We'll talk later. I just wanted you to know. Have a great lunch."

In a daze she shut the car door and heard him pull away. She tottered to the door and knocked on the shiny lion's-head knocker. This was the kind of door that could afford one of Carl's knockers, she realized.

The door was opened promptly by a uniformed maid. "Good afternoon, miss."

"Good afternoon. I'm Alexandra Drake."

"Come in, please. Mrs. Pendegraff is expecting you." The woman had a Polish accent. From a working-class half-Polish family herself, she suspected she'd have a lot more in common with this woman than with the WASP down the hall.

The maid led Lexy past exquisite paintings and antiques and into a salon where Sarah Pendegraff awaited her.

"Lexy dear, how nice of you to come on such short notice," Sarah Pendegraff said, rising gracefully from a pretty little writing desk where she'd been penning a note. It was a vision out of an era gone by.

She gave Lexy a quick hug scented with Joy, and led the way to a pair of floral chintz sofas. Her dress was also a soft floral print and there were bowls of roses throughout the room.

After pouring out two sherries into tiny crystal glasses, she said, "I'm so glad you could come today. Normally I wouldn't have lunch at this hour, but after being out until all hours I thought a late meal would be more appropriate."

"Yes. Thank you again for last night. It was a wonderful evening."

"Mmm. I was just writing a thank-you note to Florence Grayson. The trouble is finding something fresh to say about an event one attends every year. The flowers, I suppose, they were certainly different."

"Yes." Should she have sent a thank-you note to Charlie's mother? What with thefts and attempted murders she really hadn't had a moment to keep up her social correspondence.

"I, um, this is a lovely home," she managed.

"Thank you. I've always liked it. Of course, it's getting too big for me now, but I plan to live here and keep it up until Charlie settles down. Then I'll move into an apartment I own on 83rd."

She smiled. "Well, you're obviously important to Charlie and that makes you important to me. I thought we should get to know each other."

His words echoed freshly in her head. *I love you.* Not exactly words she'd imagined she'd hear from him, and definitely not after they'd known each other only a few days. If he'd intended to rock her world, he'd definitely done it.

"May I ask you a somewhat personal question?" Lexy asked.

"Of course you can. Ask me anything."

"Am I like Charlie's other girlfriends?"

"Hmm. That's not a terribly easy question to answer. You're very beautiful, of course, which I must say all his women have been. You're also hardworking and ambitious, which probably about half of his women have been."

It sounded like a cast of thousands had come before her. As though his mother read her thoughts she said, "But I'll tell you one way in which you're different. He's never been in love with any of them."

"He told you he's in love with me?" She almost croaked the words.

"Yes. But he didn't have to. I could see it when he looked at you last night."

Sarah sipped her sherry. "And pardon me if this is too personal, but I saw it when you looked at him, too."

"Oh, but, I'm...I mean. You did?"

"Maybe it was a mother's fond hope, but yes, I did."

"I, this is all so... We haven't known each other very long."

"I'm not sure you need to. Love isn't something you can plan or schedule. It doesn't happen when it's convenient or you're the right age, or your partner has the correct pedigree. Love happens in entirely inappropriate and glorious ways." She laughed. "Not that I have a great deal of personal experience, of course. The only man I ever loved was my husband. Charlie's father. Charlie's a lot like him."

"I doubt it."

"Why? Because he's a thief?"

Her eyes bugged open and she almost dropped her sherry glass down her brand-new Gucci wrap dress. She'd even run into one of the boutiques that carried some of her costume jewelry so she could wear one of her own pieces to give her confidence. Dropping her drink down her front wouldn't do much to keep up the image, but she was so shocked she could barely hang on to the thing. "You know about that?"

"Of course. We don't have a huge number of secrets

from each other, Charlie and I. Perhaps it's because he's an only child, but we've always been close." She sighed. "Of course, it's never a mother's dream, but honestly, dear, I think larceny is in the blood."

"In the blood?" This conversation was taking the most extraordinary turn.

"Yes. We can trace our family back quite far. On my side, we were pirates," she said with relish.

"Pirates? Like Johnny Depp pirates?"

"A little more bloodthirsty than that, I believe. My many times great-grandmother was a well-born young lady expected to make a great marriage. When returning from her convent school to her parents' home in France, the ship she was on was attacked by pirates. Her kidnapper was the son of a deposed duke, there were so many in those days, who'd been stripped of everything. So, the son turned to piracy and did quite well for himself, if you disregard the price on his head and the fact that he couldn't turn up in decent society without immediately being taken out and hanged."

"My goodness."

"Well, my many times great-grandmother, whose name was Veronique, by the way, and the pirate fell in love. It's an extraordinary story because he actually escorted her to her home, in spite of the price on his head. She was completely unharmed and quite determined to marry him. When they got to her home, he formally asked for her hand in marriage. Of course, her family was so relieved to have her returned to them that they almost agreed on the spot. But he was a pirate and a rascal and she was their only daughter so they said that if he could reestablish his reputation, he could have her."

"Lunch is served, Mrs. Pendegraff."

"Ah, thank you, Sophia."

The women moved into the dining room, which had been laid for two.

"I thought something simple. It's just salads and quiche. Is that all right?"

"Oh, it's perfect."

When they were seated, Lexy said, "So, what happened to your many times great-grandmother and the pirate?"

"It's like a fairy tale, really. He had so much money that he could afford to buy a pardon from the Pope and then he bought himself a nice estate in France and renewed his addresses. Veronique had, by this time, made it clear that she wasn't interested in any other man, so they were allowed to marry. It was a very successful marriage, by all accounts, and they had twelve children."

"Twelve children?"

"Veronique wrote about her adventures in a diary, which was passed down through the family. That's how I know so much about her. Anyway, on my side at least, there's historical evidence of thievery. So, when Charlie went into the business, I had to wonder if it was hereditary." She passed a bread basket to Lexy. "Of course, all that's behind him now."

"Are you sure?"

"As much as I can be. I think he was bored more than anything. His father was a truly wonderful man and a brilliant lawyer. I think Charlie felt that he couldn't compete and, as boys are wont to do, decided to do whatever was the opposite of what his father wanted for him."

"He couldn't have become a used car dealer or a stockbroker or something?"

The older woman smiled. "Charlie tends to go all out when he puts his mind to something."

"So I've noticed."

Lunch was surprisingly pleasant after that. There was something about a woman admitting her family tree contained thieves and pirates that encouraged intimacy. They discussed jewelry, food and fashion. They were enjoying coffee when Sophia entered the room.

"Excuse me for interrupting, but Florence Grayson is on the phone. She says it is urgent."

"Florence Grayson? Good heavens. Whatever can she want? Do you mind if I take it, Lexy?"

"No. Of course not." But internal alarms were going off. Why was Florence Grayson phoning Charlie's mother? And where was the murderous Mr. G.?

The phone conversation made its meandering way through the evening before, compliments were exchanged, while Lexy wished Charlie were here. How could she tell his mother that one of her oldest friends was married to a psychopath?

She tried not to eavesdrop, but it was impossible not to when she heard her own name. "Lexy?" Sarah Pendegraff's voice trailed upward in surprise.

Lexy waved her hands, "No," but Charlie's mother was busy fixing one of the blooms in the rose bowl in the middle of the table and didn't see her. "As a matter of fact she's here now. We were enjoying a late lunch."

Only then did she glance up at Lexy and must have read horror in her face. "But unfortunately she's about to leave. Yes, of course, I'll tell her. All right. Thank you again for a lovely party last night. Goodbye."

She hung up and turned to Lexy. "Florence Grayson would like you to call her at your earliest convenience."

"Did she say why?"

"No. Florence sounded odd. She seemed very anxious to talk to you. In fact, now I think about it, she was rather strange last night when she first met you. I—" She slapped a perfectly manicured hand over her mouth. "Whatever is wrong with me? Forgive me, dear. I feel I've been horribly gauche. Never mind. I've put her off, now. Told her you're about to leave."

But Lexy was still puzzling over the woman's odd comments. "Gauche? Why would you think you were being gauche? Mrs. Grayson did act strangely when she met me, but—" Then the obvious conclusion came to her. If Charlie knew about Grayson's mistress, she supposed a woman as plugged into the social network as his mother obviously was would be bound to know that the man had a wandering eye.

"Oh." Lexy felt herself becoming flustered. She had Charlie telling her he was in love with her, his mother thinking she'd had an affair with Grayson, the man's wife wanting to talk to her. This really was the craziest day. "If you're thinking that Mr. Grayson and I...um, knew each other, well, no. I never met him before last night."

She fidgeted in her chair. Glanced at the French ormolu clock atop the marble mantel. Where was Charlie? "I'm hoping when your son gets here he can explain everything."

She didn't like the feeling of vulnerability that possessed her. Here she was in a house she didn't know with an older woman who seemed more adept at flower arranging than self-defense and the wife of a murderous criminal knew where she was. If Florence happened to mention to her husband that Lexy was here, what was to stop the man from sending his thugs to try to get at her?

Charlie said he'd arranged security, but she still felt a little nervous. A scratching sound at the window had her jumping out of her seat and assuming a defensive posture. She wasn't going down without a fight.

"Lexy. What's wrong? It's only Buttons, my cat."

Before her bemused gaze, a sleek Siamese slinked its way from the window into the room. "You're not allergic, are you?"

"No." She took a slow, deliberate breath and sat back down feeling incredibly foolish. "I'm a little jumpy, that's all."

Charlie's mother regarded her steadily. "Perhaps you'd better tell me what's going on?"

"You won't like it."

Sarah smiled slowly. "Then we'd better take coffee back in the sitting room."

They'd barely got their coffees when Sophia's voice was heard in the hall, coming toward them, a man answered her and Lexy wilted with relief. Charlie was here. Somehow he made her feel that everything would be all right. On her own, she felt overwhelmed by all that was going on, but with the two of them working as a team, she felt like they could do anything.

The door opened. "Mr. Grayson, ma'am."

22

"OH, NO," Lexy said, and without conscious thought, rose and went to stand by Charlie's mother's side determined to protect the woman to the best of her ability.

Grayson entered and if his reddened cheeks and frantic eyes gave away his agitation, she could see that he was trying to hold on to his facade of composure. "I'm so sorry to trouble you, Sarah, but Florence left word that she was on her way here and I must speak to her about something important."

"You two can't afford cell phones?" Lexy snapped.

He blinked at her, then made a helpless gesture with hands that shook slightly. "I know it's silly, but neither of us can bear them. At a time like this, it would be useful, though. It's really very important that I find her." He glanced around the room as though his wife might be hiding behind a piece of furniture. "You're sure you haven't seen her?"

"No," Sarah said. "She telephoned earlier, but obviously, it's not convenient for me to have a visitor. I'm having lunch with Alexandra."

"Yes. Of course. I'm so sorry to bother you." He

scratched at his face and she could see the bulge of a hive. "If she shows up, will you let me know?"

"Yes. Certainly."

As he turned, the door behind him was thrust open and Charlie appeared. "Oh, thank God," Lexy murmured, feeling somehow that everything would be all right now Charlie was here. His gaze took in the scene at a glance and settled on hers. The smile in his eyes was relieved, intimate.

"What are you doing here?" he demanded of Grayson, maneuvering his body so that he was between the man and the two women.

"Not that it's any of your business, but I am looking for my wife."

The man looked as though he wanted to say more, but ended up turning slowly toward the door. Which opened again before he reached it.

Mrs. Grayson flew in the room. Her eyes were wild, her hair askew.

"Florence, thank heaven."

"Don't you Florence me." The woman opened her purse, one of those with designer logos printed all over it that Lexy always found tacky. She pulled out a mass of gold and green and just as Lexy realized it was the necklace, she squeezed her fist around the gems and threw the jewelry at Lexy.

Transfixed, they all watched the flash of diamond, emerald and the duller shine of gold as the necklace sailed through the air. Reflexively Lexy grabbed it before it could fall to the floor.

"You bitch!" the woman screamed. "You've ruined everything."

"Florence, dear, please," her husband said in a soothing tone. More hives had broken out on his face in bright red raised patches.

"Don't you talk to me, you sniveling fool. It's not the right necklace. She switched it." And the woman broke down into tears.

Edward Grayson patted his sobbing wife awkwardly on the shoulder but she shook him off.

"My wife's very upset. You see, she believes you've got her necklace. It's very important to her. Sentimental value and all that."

Charlie and Lexy exchanged another glance.

Charlie moved closer to Edward. "You must be pretty surprised to see Lexy and me alive."

"Of course I'm not. I saw you last night. You both appeared perfectly healthy."

"Yeah. That was before your thugs came in and stole the necklace and tried to kill us. If you're here to finish the job, you're wasting your time."

"I don't believe it's stealing to retrieve your own property. If there's a thief in this room, Pendegraff, it's you."

"Retired thief," Charlie corrected him.

Mrs. Grayson was sobbing quietly into her hands. "The necklace was mine. Why did he take it?"

Sarah moved to her old friend. "Can I get you something, Florence? Coffee? A glass of water perhaps?"

The distraught woman nodded and allowed herself to be led to the sofa and gently seated. Charlie's mother poured water from a pitcher on a side table. Lexy imagined the Polish servant keeping the water refreshed all day so it was always fresh. Like the rose bowls.

Sarah pressed the glass into Florence Grayson's hand.

"Thank you," the woman whispered and sipped her drink.

"I didn't take your necklace, Mrs. Grayson. I was hired to steal it back. Your husband hired me. But he also hired thugs to kill me, kill Lexy and take the necklace back by force. Why would you do that, Grayson? Why?"

"I don't know what you're talking about. Why would I want to kill you? I wanted the gems back quietly."

"And you wanted a certain young woman who stole them disposed of quietly, didn't you?"

Grayson was scratching at his face again. He jerked his chin at his wife and then shook his head violently. "Don't know what you're talking about."

"Lexy crafted the second necklace. It was enough to fool your henchmen, wasn't it? When they broke into our suite and stole it. But they tried to finish their handiwork, didn't they? Shot up the bed where they thought we were sleeping?"

"What?" his mother gasped, putting a hand to her heart.

"No." Grayson jerked the word out. "All I want is my property back. That was the original necklace she was wearing last night. Where is it?" He shot a glance at his distraught wife. "It belongs to me. I want it back."

"That necklace is your ticket to jail."

"Do not pass Go. Do not collect two hundred," Lexy added.

"Putting your mistress's body in Lexy's place wasn't too smart. The cops will connect the dots easily."

"Stop. Please. Ladies present."

"Oh, come on, Grayson. Drop the act. You let your girlfriend try on the famous Isabella Emeralds and she took a liking to them, didn't she? Maybe you got tired of her so she decided to give herself a little goodbye present…is that what happened?"

"No." The man was frantic, gesturing to his wife again and again. "This is nonsense. I don't have a mistress."

Lexy took up the interrogation. If they could get Grayson to admit what he'd done in front of witnesses, they had him. "Everybody in town knows about your infidelities. I'm sure your wife's always known. Wives always do." She sent Charlie a steely-eyed look. "Which is why I don't recommend the practice. If you're interested."

His implacable expression softened. "Noted. And not planning on it."

Maybe this was a strange time for her to realize she was as much in love with Charlie as he could possibly be with her but the truth hit her with a solid punch. "Good." Something zapped between them, a spooky unspoken communication that no greeting card could ever duplicate. If she had to put it into words it would be something like, "I love you. Back at you. We're in this together. We're going to make it."

But of course no words were spoken, the entire exchange took place in a millisecond and then Charlie turned his attention back to Grayson. "The body found in Lexy's studio, the female body burned beyond recognition? It's already been ID'd by the cops. It's Tiffany Starr."

Grayson made a strange gurgling sound in the back of his throat, like he'd choked on his own spit.

"Stop it," Florence suddenly screamed. "Don't mention that horrible name to me."

She jerked to her feet and to Lexy's horror, she saw that from her handbag, the woman had taken out a gun. And she was pointing it right at Lexy.

"Florence, sweetheart, what are you doing?"

"You're so stupid you never did figure it out, did you? You're all stupid." Her eyes were wet and haggard but also gleaming with madness. "Did you really think I didn't know? I found your pictures of your little girlfriend wearing my necklace. My necklace! She was naked. It was the most disgusting thing I'd ever seen. I couldn't let her live after that."

"You killed Tiffany?"

"Sure. And I hired my own people to make sure I got the necklace back and that nobody who handled it would live to talk about it."

"But—"

"Quiet. Now, Edward, you and Charlie are going to get the real necklace. If I get it back, then you're free to go. If I don't get it back in one hour, Lexy dies." She glanced at Charlie's mother. "Sorry, Sarah, but I'll have to kill you, too. Nothing personal."

Charlie was rigid. Ever since the gun had appeared she'd felt his coiled tension, his readiness to spring. All he needed was an opening. But Mrs. Grayson wasn't giving him one. And Lexy was cursing herself all over the place for being so focused on the husband she hadn't noticed the wife pulling a gun until it was too late.

"You don't want to do this, Florence," Charlie's mother said in the soothing voice she'd probably use on a toddler having a tantrum. "You'll never be able to host another of your lovely Diamond Balls if you kill my son and Alexandra Drake. Why don't we put the weapon down. I'll get Sophia to make us a pot of tea and we'll discuss this sensibly. I'm sure, if the necklace is yours, that Charlie will get it for you, won't you, Charlie?"

"Yes, Mother," he said.

"I don't want tea, I want my necklace. And if I don't

get it in one hour, Charlie, I will shoot Alexandra and then your mother! Do I make myself clear?"

"Florence, please," her husband begged.

The gun made a definitive and deadly sound as she released the safety. "Fifty-nine minutes. And with my low blood sugar I'll start to shake. You really don't want my trigger finger getting shaky."

"No, dear. Of course not."

"You try anything, anything at all, and Lexy dies. I've killed before. I'll do it again."

Once more Lexy and Charlie shared a glance. He was telling her to stay calm and not try anything to overpower her captor. She was telling him to be careful. Oh, yeah, and that she loved him.

"I'll be back," he said aloud. "Don't worry."

She nodded.

"I'm sorry, Mom," he said, turning to Sarah.

"We'll be fine," she assured him.

Grayson and Charlie turned to the door and Lexy realized that Grayson didn't have a gun or any kind of weapon. Florence must believe that her threat to kill Lexy and Charlie's mother was all the incentive he needed.

And maybe it was, but Lexy had finally found the person who was responsible for destroying her business, her home and who had used her gun to commit a murder. She didn't intend to stand by and let Charlie walk back into the gun sights of a madwoman.

Not if she could help it.

Grayson opened the door and held it for Charlie, as though they were two old friends lunching at their club. The gesture was so automatic, and so absolutely foreign to what was going on in this bright, rose-scented room that she could barely take it in.

As the door opened, a large bulk in a flak jacket barreled in, a series of dark shadowed figures behind him, all holding semiautomatic weapons.

"Hold your fire," Charlie shouted frantically, turning and diving to protect Lexy.

After the first second of startled realization that the security guys had followed the tracking device in the necklace, she threw herself to the floor, grabbing Florence Grayson's feet—encased in Chanel pumps—and yanking them out from under her in a move she'd learned years ago from her father.

The woman screamed with rage. She felt her try to focus her aim, but in a blur, a floral-print angel of vengeance grabbed her gun arm and shoved it upward, so the shot that rang out hit the crystal chandelier.

A sparkling glitter, like a cache of enormous diamonds, rained down onto Edward Grayson before he could jump out of the way.

As Florence Grayson fell back onto the sofa, trying to tug the gun away from his mother, Charlie got hold of her wrist and wrested the firearm from her clawlike grasp.

"My necklace," she panted. "I want my necklace," she shouted as a burly guy shoved her arms into handcuffs.

"You okay, Mom?" Charlie asked.

"Yes. Fine."

He then tumbled to the floor. Cradled Lexy in his arms. "Hey, how you doing?"

"It's been quite a day."

He kissed her and she clung to him, feeling the emotion pulse between them. She kissed him back, hungry, urgent, knowing how close they'd come to disaster, possibly even death, and celebrating the fact that they were still so vitally alive.

"It's not every day I tell a woman I love her," he said against her lips.

She smoothed back his hair, looked up into his eyes.

"It's not every day I tell a man I love him back."

"Really?"

"Hell, yeah."

Epilogue

THANKS TO THE ISABELLA EMERALDS, the Manhattan auction house was packed.

After Florence and Edward Grayson's arrests, it had been determined that, while he had originally hired Charlie to steal the necklace back, it was Florence who had killed Tiffany Starr. Florence had hired the thugs who'd tried to kill them, who'd burned down Lexy's studio and who'd broken into their hotel suite and stolen the copy of the Isabella Emeralds and once more tried to kill Charlie and Lexy.

Now, Edward was raising the money for his wife's defense. In a nice twist of justice, Edward Grayson was auctioning the Isabella Emeralds to pay her team of top-notch lawyers. Ironically the burst of publicity as the story hit the media only upped the estimated value of the ancient jewels.

Grayson was going to need all the money he could raise, too, since it turned out that Tiffany's accomplice, the older woman who'd masqueraded as Florence Grayson, had been hiding in Tiffany's apartment when Florence came by for a visit. The woman's testimony that her young friend had been kidnapped by a gun-wielding

Florence Grayson would go a long way to putting the murderous Mrs. behind bars for a long time.

Lexy and Charlie didn't buy the necklace, but they were present at the auction where it was sold. After spirited bidding among collectors from London, Frankfurt, Kuwait and New York, the winner was a museum in Spain.

"Very appropriate," Charlie said, as he and Lexy walked home arm in arm. "Now everyone can enjoy the Isabella Emeralds."

"And I guess they are home where they belong."

"It's finally over."

They hadn't talked about the future and she felt silly bringing it up. So far they were happy; she'd been spending her days in her new studio and her nights at Charlie's place.

Amanda was back as her assistant and, if anything, seemed to be more focused. She was certainly happier than Lexy had ever seen her. She and Healey were an odd couple, but so far their relationship was working. After spending two weeks in the Caribbean, they'd returned tanned and happy. Amanda had removed the ring from her eyebrow, and sported a tiny new tatt: a tiny bird flying above the sailboat, which seemed to have some kind of personal significance since twice she'd caught Healey placing his lips there when he thought no one was looking.

Lexy liked Amanda's way with customers, her artistic eye and was already thinking of promoting her to assistant designer and hiring someone else to take over the retail part of the operation.

Amazingly her business had never been better. She supposed that since her fame had increased due to the

Isabella Emeralds and the murder trial, she shouldn't be surprised that her business was booming.

Charlie halted her, turned her to face him and kissed her. He did that a lot. As though he couldn't wait until they were back at his place and had privacy.

She put a hand to his cheek. How she loved this tough, tender man.

"Now I've got my new studio up and running, I should really think about getting my own apartment."

"You could do that."

Her heart fell a little. It wasn't that she didn't know she couldn't stay with him forever, but it would be nice to have him argue with her.

"Or you could marry me."

Her jaw dropped. "What?"

He pulled out a jewelry box. "I know this is kind of strange, since you probably figured you'd design our rings. But this is a family ring. Jeez, I'm totally blowing this already." He took a breath and she realized he was nervous.

"Lexy, will you marry me?"

He opened the box and she saw an exquisite diamond solitaire, an art deco design that she fell in love with on sight. "Oh, Charlie. Are you sure?"

"Are you kidding me? Ever since I kidnapped you, I've known I was never going to let you go."

"That pirate blood really does run through your veins, doesn't it?"

"I promise that you are the last thing I'm stealing. From now on, I'm an honest businessman. So, will you?"

"I don't know. My dad's a cop. He might freak out that I'm marrying a thief. Even if you are a reformed thief."

Charlie wrinkled his face, like he was in pain. "I have to tell you something and you probably won't like it."

"What?"

"I already asked your father for permission to marry you."

She jerked her head up and stared at him in growing wrath. "You did what?"

"I asked your father for your hand in marriage. A month ago. I told him I used to be a thief. He took the news pretty well, but he made me wait a month and then ask him again. So, I did. Yesterday, when the two of us went for a beer, I asked for his permission to marry you. And he said yes."

"You're just doing this for hot sex, aren't you?"

"What are you talking about?"

"I know you. You're getting me mad so then we can have hot makeup sex."

Charlie threw back his head and laughed. "Yep, that's exactly what I'm doing. And after the hot makeup sex, what do you say to trying out 'will you marry me?' sex."

A sudden lump of emotion clogged her throat but she managed a cocky grin. "I've never tried that. I bet it's hot."

"Especially if you say yes."

He nibbled her lower lip while she ran her hands up and down his back. Sometimes, she realized, you just knew. In the same spooky way she could look at gemstones and know instantly what their setting should be, so could she realize at this moment that she and Charlie were meant to be together forever.

"Yes, Charles Pendegraff III, I will marry you."

He pushed the ring on her finger and she wasn't a

bit surprised to find it was a perfect fit. "I love you, Lexy."

"I love you, too." They continued on, hand in hand, the diamond sparkling on her ring finger. "So, if I'm going to marry you, I guess I should know what your favorite sexual position is."

He grinned. "Let's get home and I'll show you."

* * * * *

*Harlequin offers a romance for every mood!
See below for a sneak peek
from our paranormal romance line,
Silhouette® Nocturne™.
Enjoy a preview of REUNION by USA TODAY
bestselling author Lindsay McKenna.*

Aella closed her eyes and sensed a distinct shift, like
movement from the world around her to the unseen
world.

She opened her eyes. And had a slight shock at the
man standing ten feet away. He wasn't just any man. Her
heart leaped and pounded. He reminded her of a fierce
warrior from an ancient civilization. Incan? She wasn't
sure but she felt his deep power and masculinity.

I'm Aella. Are you the guardian of this sacred site?
she asked, hoping her telepathy was strong.

Fox's entire body soared with joy. Fox struggled to
put his personal pleasure aside.

*Greetings, Aella. I'm the assistant guardian to this
sacred area. You may call me Fox. How can I be of
service to you, Aella?* he asked.

*I'm searching for a green sphere. A legend says that
the Emperor Pachacuti had seven emerald spheres created for the Emerald Key necklace. He had seven of his
priestesses and priests travel the world to hide these
spheres from evil forces. It is said that when all seven
spheres are found, restrung and worn, that Light will
return to the Earth. The fourth sphere is here, at your
sacred site. Are you aware of it?* Aella held her breath.
She loved looking at him, especially his sensual mouth.
The desire to kiss him came out of nowhere.

Fox was stunned by the request. *I know of the Emerald Key necklace because I served the emperor at the time it was created. However, I did not realize that one of the spheres is here.*

Aella felt sad. Why? Every time she looked at Fox, her heart felt as if it would tear out of her chest. *May I stay in touch with you as I work with this site?* she asked.

Of course. Fox wanted nothing more than to be here with her. To absorb her ephemeral beauty and hear her speak once more.

Aella's spirit lifted. What *was* this strange connection between them? Her curiosity was strong, but she had more pressing matters. In the next few days, Aella knew her life would change forever. How, she had no idea....

Look for REUNION
by USA TODAY bestselling author
Lindsay McKenna,
available April 2010, only from
Silhouette® Nocturne™.

HARLEQUIN®

INTRIGUE®

WILL THIS REUNITED FAMILY
BE STRONG ENOUGH TO EXPOSE
A LURKING KILLER?

FIND OUT IN THIS ALL-NEW
THRILLING TRILOGY FROM TOP
HARLEQUIN INTRIGUE AUTHOR

B.J. DANIELS

WHITEHORSE
MONTANA

Winchester Ranch

GUN-SHY BRIDE—*April 2010*

HITCHED—*May 2010*

TWELVE-GAUGE GUARDIAN—
June 2010

Silhouette

Desire

OLIVIA GATES

BILLIONAIRE, M.D.

Dr. Rodrigo Valderrama has it all…
everything but the woman he's secretly
desired and despised. A woman forbidden
to him—his brother's widow.
And she's pregnant.

Cybele was injured in a plane crash
and lost her memory. All she knows is
she's falling for the doctor who has swept her
away to his estate to heal. If only the secrets
in his eyes didn't promise to tear
them forever apart.

Available March wherever you buy books.

Always Powerful, Passionate and Provocative.

REQUEST YOUR FREE BOOKS!

**2 FREE NOVELS
PLUS 2
FREE GIFTS!**

HARLEQUIN®

Blaze

Red-hot reads!

HARLEQUIN® *Romance*®

ROMANCE, RIVALRY
AND A FAMILY REUNITED

THE BRIDES
of
BELLA ROSA

William Valentine and his beloved wife, Lucia, live
a beautiful life together, but when his former love Rosa
and the secret family they had together resurface,
an instant rivalry is formed. Can these families
get through the past and come together as one?

Step into the world of Bella Rosa
beginning this April with

Beauty and the Reclusive Prince
by
RAYE MORGAN

Eight volumes to collect and treasure!

www.eHarlequin.com

HR17650

COMING NEXT MONTH

Available March 30, 2010

#531 JUST FOOLING AROUND
Encounters
Julie Kenner and Kathleen O'Reilly

#532 THE DRIFTER
Smooth Operators
Kate Hoffmann

#533 WHILE SHE WAS SLEEPING...
The Wrong Bed: Again and Again
Isabel Sharpe

#534 THE CAPTIVE
Blaze Historicals
Joanne Rock

#535 UNDER HIS SPELL
Forbidden Fantasies
Kathy Lyons

#536 DELICIOUSLY DANGEROUS
Undercover Lovers
Karen Anders

www.eHarlequin.com